Sons of Gold and Fire

GOLD AND FIRE

FRED PHILLIPS

Copyright

Dedication

For my mom, who instilled a love of words at a young age; my son, who unknowingly inspired Aron's optimism; and my wife, who convinced me the story was good enough to send out into the world.

Contents

He wore a dark cloak, and the shadows in the room seemed to gather deeply around him

Prologue

Sons of Gold and Fire
By Fred Phillips

PROLOGUE

The commander glanced around nervously as he stood outside the heavy wooden door that hid his fate. He wanted to run away, but the well-armed guards to either side and behind him made that an impossibility. Why had he come back here? He could have fled like so many of the men and goblins under his charge, lost himself in the wider world. He'd considered it, but deep down, he'd known there would be no running away. The wizard didn't care about most men or goblins, but he was a commanding officer. Their master needed someone to answer for the failure, and there would be no rest for him if he fled.

One of the guards knocked at the door. A few tense moments

passed, then they heard a click, and the door cracked open, seemingly on its own. The man who had knocked pushed it wider and shoved the commander hurriedly through. He heard the door thump closed solidly behind him. He shivered at the sound, like a bell tolling his impending doom.

A small silver candelabra burned on a table in the center of the room, providing the only source of light and casting shadows around the edges. On the far side, a figure stood staring out a window into the night. Few people in the army had met the man who issued their orders, and even fewer had lived to tell the tale. He wore a dark cloak, and the shadows in the room seemed to gather deeply around him. In the meager light, the commander caught a quick glance of long, pale hair—blonde or white perhaps—before the wizard reached behind him and raised the hood over his head. He turned then.

The commander dropped to a knee before his master, bowing so low that he nearly kissed the stone floor. He did not look up.

"You led our forces in the north?" The voice that spoke from the shadowy hood chilled the room. He sounded as refined and proper as a lord, but the tone held not an ounce of humanity.

"Yes, milord."

"Did I not provide you with a great army—beasts and men —many times the size that should have been needed to defeat the smattering of farmers and gatherers that stood in your way?"

It hadn't really been a question, but he answered anyway, "You did, milord."

"Then, can you explain to me why I do not rule everything north of the mountains today?"

The commander attempted to control his fearful trembling

and keep his voice steady as he answered. If he were to die today, he would not humiliate himself. "There were unforeseen circumstances, milord."

"Unforeseen circumstances…" The wizard paused, and the tension in the room mounted until it was almost unbearable. "Tell me."

"A creature that shouldn't exist. Something out of children's stories. I've never seen such power. It was a terror. There was no stopping it. It burned and clawed and destroyed."

The words tumbled out of his mouth in a rush. The wizard snorted.

"I don't want to hear children's tales."

The commander's eyes widened as he felt something pushing its way into his head. He fought to block it, but there was no keeping the wizard out of his mind. Sheer terror overtook him, and he let out a strangled sound. A second later, he went quiet and the light faded from his eyes.

"Now, commander, show me exactly what you saw."

He couldn't resist as his master shuffled through his thoughts and memories.

"Gold and fire, milord." The commander's voice was flat and dead as he said it. "Gold and Fire."

One

Aron circled his opponent warily, eyes darting left, right, up, and down, searching for any sort of opening where he could strike. The larger man smiled and lunged, sword snaking toward his chest. Aron backpedaled from the attack, slapping at his opponent's blade with his own. He barely managed to keep it at bay and stay on his feet. A quick twisting motion from his attacker, and the boy's sword was driven wide, leaving his torso open. With a wicked grin, the man turned his own blade and drove it hard into Aron's ribs. The breath blasted out of him as the sword made impact, and he fell to his knees, gasping for air.

"Yield." He just managed to croak out the word before his opponent could strike another blow.

Sir Gareth Rayne shook his head and reached down to give his squire a hand up.

"Defense, boy." It was a familiar refrain from his teacher. "You're too focused on striking your own blow. If your enemy realizes that, he will make short work of you. Battles are not all attacks and glory. You should never be surprised by an offensive move when you are looking at your opponent."

Aron winced as he pulled himself to his feet. That blow was going to leave a bruise despite the padded armor they wore for their daily sparring sessions. In the two years he'd been training with the knight, he had learned that Sir Gareth was not nearly as gentle or caring as Commander Devan had been during his first lessons back in Lanfield. He'd made the mistake of complaining about Gareth's rough ways only once.

"If you want to be coddled, go home to your mother and raise your sheep," the knight told him. That jab had hurt more than any blow he'd delivered with the sword. "My job is to make sure you stay alive, not to make you comfortable."

The knight had been true to his word. There was absolutely nothing comfortable about serving under Sir Gareth. He wasn't a cruel master, but he was hard and demanding. He was well respected among the King's Knights, and he wouldn't be embarrassed by a squire who wasn't up to his standards.

Aron stretched himself a bit and then reached down to pick the wooden sword up out of the dirt.

"I believe that's enough for today," Gareth said.

Aron ignored the knight, raising the sword into the

defensive position from which they started their training. The boy was embarrassed and angry. He would get this right. He must. Gareth studied him thoughtfully for a moment, then raised his own wooden blade in front of him in salute.

"As you wish." Before the words were completely out of the knight's mouth, he burst into a sudden attack that had Aron entirely on the defensive and immediately outmatched. It was over in seconds. The boy found himself face down in the dirt, his sword several feet away, and his rear stinging from the blow the blade master landed there.

Aron's face twisted in rage as he reached out for his sword and began to push himself up out of the dust. He felt Gareth's foot on his still-stinging rear, pushing him gently back to the ground.

"Stay down, Aron." His voice was stern. "Calm yourself. Anger and pride are a losing strategy. Pride is what earned you the shame I now see in your face. Anger will make it worse. If you go into battle behind a shield of rage, you will lose. It's not the first time that emotion has gotten you into trouble, is it?"

The knight removed his foot, stepped back, and raised his sword. Aron rolled to his back and picked up his own weapon. Gareth was correct, of course. His rage had caused him serious trouble when he'd gone to Lanfield to plead for his place among the knights. In fact, it had almost gotten him killed. That didn't make it any easier to hear.

"My advice to you is yield the day and spend the rest of the afternoon pondering this lesson. The choice is yours, but if you choose to continue and come at me with anger, I will not be so gentle with you. This is a lesson you must learn."

Aron stewed as he stared up at his mentor. He wanted nothing more than to prove the man wrong, but he also knew that the knight meant every word he'd just said. If Aron continued to fight, he'd regret it even more than he already did. His behind still burned, and the injury to his ribs was stiffening up. He blew out a long, ragged breath and sagged.

"I yield."

Gareth smiled at him then, the stern taskmaster of a few minutes before disappearing. He reached down and helped Aron to his feet.

"I know these are hard lessons for you," he said. "But they are vital. You are not a knight, nor are you a match for any man in the king's service...yet. And, believe me, there are many that will challenge your position and won't stop at simply bruising your body and your pride. I admire your drive and will, and it may one day make you great. But you still have a lot to learn."

They'd had this conversation many times. He'd also had it with Devan. The small unit of knights that now protected the villages north of the mountain were handpicked by Devan and Gareth, and they were much different from those he'd find when he had to return to Lanfield. Out here, birthright didn't matter much. In the city, it would be everything. Most of the other squires of the King's Knights were young nobles who wouldn't welcome a simple farmer into their ranks. Thankfully, it would be a couple of years before Aron had to deal with that. Devan and Gareth had agreed that he wouldn't be sent for his training in Lanfield until his master felt that he was ready. At this rate, he might never get there.

He'd been training with Gareth for nearly two years since Commander Devan Kyle had convinced King James that a garrison was needed in the north to protect against the goblins and whoever or whatever was driving them against the villages. Aron had been the hero of that battle, bringing a weapon that the goblins and their masters were no match against—the great golden dragon Doubloon, his friend. He didn't feel much like a hero now, though, as he limped away from the training grounds. He missed his days in Doubloon's valley and soaring above the mountains on the dragon's back. He missed his friend. But Doubloon was just as uncomfortable around humans as they were around him.

A firm hand on his shoulder pulled him out of his maudlin memories. He looked up into the face of his mentor, which had softened quite a bit from their training session.

"I know you still question whether you belong among the King's Knights." He stared hard into Aron's eyes. "Do not. I trust Commander Kyle with my life, and if he says you belong, you do. I've seen it, too, in the time that I've trained you. But you will have much more to overcome than any other squire currently in the king's service. You must be prepared for that. When you go to Lanfield, you need to leave the anger behind. It will get you drummed out of the corps, or worse. Do you understand?"

Aron nodded. He did. He always had. Even from that first fight with the guards in the city, he understood it, but sometimes, he just couldn't help himself.

"Now, go get cleaned up and spend the rest of the afternoon practicing your meditation exercises. I believe they'll help you far more than combat training."

With that, Sir Gareth turned and went about his other duties, leaving his aching squire standing on the training grounds, still contemplating if he really belonged there.

Two

Aron soared among clouds on the back of his friend. He looked down on the mountains and valleys they'd explored on their regular flights during the weeks he'd lived with Doubloon. They sailed out over the forests and fields surrounding his village, and he reveled in the sight of his home from above. Then, in the distance, a dark cloud, threatening everything that he loved. The memory shook him from the peaceful meditative state.

He opened his eyes and sighed. Sir Gareth told him that mental preparation was just as important as physical preparation, and he knew it was true. But Aron struggled greatly with the meditation exercises the knight had tried to teach him. Thoughts of his time with Doubloon were about the only thing that led him to that peaceful place Gareth wanted him to find, but those same memories were usually also what pulled him out of it.

He hadn't seen the golden dragon in nearly two years, not since Doubloon had reluctantly revealed himself to the humans of the village in order to protect Aron's family and friends. The dragon had routed the goblin army that had been marching on the village, then disappeared back into the mountains, Aron assumed to the hidden valley where they first met.

He missed the peaceful valley, with its green meadows and clear stream filled with fish. He missed his long chats with Doubloon about things great and small. He missed their flights through the mountains and the crisp, cold air in his face. Most of all, though, he missed his friend. They'd known each other only a short time, but they had developed a bond, and Aron's heart ached in his absence. His mind wandered often, just as it had before his trip to Lanfield; only now, the thoughts were not about slaying dragons, but rather about what his friend might be doing. He wondered often if Doubloon longed for his company as well, or if the dragon was glad to be rid of his human burden.

Several times, Aron had reached out, calling in his mind for Doubloon, but there had been no answer. He'd been tempted to use the dragon's final gift to him, the golden amulet that encased the ruby scale of Doubloon's father. It remained secret and safely hidden, just as the dragon had told him, stuffed into the bottom of the chest that Devan had gifted him to hold the gear of a squire of the King's Knights. But Doubloon had also told him to use it only during a time of great need, and he didn't think that simply missing his friend qualified, even though it felt that way sometimes.

Aron stared at the walls of the small sanctuary that all the knights used for meditation and reflection. Though they'd hung tapestries around the building and placed a plush rug in the center of the floor, it clearly remained a converted tool shed. It was a perfect metaphor for how Aron felt. For all that he longed to be a knight, he wondered sometimes if he were, in fact, just a plain shepherd dressed up in a fancy suit of armor.

With a sigh, he pulled himself to his feet and extinguished the sweet-smelling candles they used to set the mood for reflection. There was no use sitting here wasting more time. He wasn't cut out for meditation. A niggling thought ate at the back of his mind that maybe he wasn't cut out for the knighthood, either.

As he turned toward the door of the shed, thunderous sounds began to boom through the village. It was a noise everyone dreaded. The great bronze bells had been one of the first additions the knights made when they'd taken up residence here. They clanged with deep thuds as someone swung from the rope that hung beneath them. It warned the people of danger. They'd rung only a few times since they'd been installed, and those had been training exercises, making sure everyone knew what to do. No training was scheduled today. Aron's heart leaped into his throat. They only rang for one reason; goblins had been spotted.

He stood frozen for a moment, listening to the deep tolls of the bells, a strange mix of fear and excitement warring within him. Wasn't this what he longed for? The chance to prove his worth and protect the village? So, why was he scared to death?

He shook off his hesitation and crashed through the door of the shed and out into the chaos of the village. People ran to and fro, some with makeshift weapons heading toward the barricades that had been built around the town, others herding children and animals to relative safety at the center of the village. He quickly found Sir Gareth standing at the barricade, looking out across the field where Doubloon had destroyed the great goblin army nearly two years ago.

"Shall I fetch your armor?" Aron asked.

The knight looked at him with a grim face. "There's no time. I shouldn't need it anyway. It's just a small raiding party. My knights will make easy work of them."

"What do you want me to do?"

"Get your sword. Stand at the ready with the men of your village. If any of them get past us, it will be up to you to stop them."

Aron nodded. He felt a knot twist in his chest as he remembered his first encounter with a goblin, a wild one in the mountains. He'd killed the monster completely by accident. He was better trained now, for sure, but he also remembered how he'd felt when he first realized what he'd done. He wondered, not for the first time, if he could actually strike the killing blow again. Apparently, Sir Gareth saw the reluctance in his face.

"You'll be fine," he said. "They won't get through us, and if they do, you'll do your duty. Now, get yourself ready."

Aron turned and sprinted to the rack on the training grounds where he'd left his sword earlier. He strapped it on hastily and went to join the men of the village at the fence while the five knights who were assigned to the north rode out to face the threat.

Aron found his father among the men, the great sword that had belonged to his grandfather at his waist. His Da saw him and smiled. Aron thought he looked relieved.

"Not going out with the knights today, eh?" his father asked.

Aron shook his head. "Sir Gareth wants me to stay behind in case any of them get through."

"If they do, we'll take care of them. But I'd say it's not likely."

They looked back across the field at the small group of goblins charging hard toward them. The creatures outnumbered the knights at least four to one, but Aron had seen Sir Gareth and his men in action, and he thought his father was probably correct. The goblins didn't stand a chance.

The two tiny armies met in a cloud of dust and noise, and the fight was over almost as soon as it started. The knights sliced through the invaders like a scythe through wheat. They rode back through the opening in the barricade in a jovial mood, a few of them arguing over who had defeated the most foes. The men around Aron all breathed a sigh of relief and joined in the celebration, congratulating the knights on their impressive victory.

The joy was shattered by the sound of a very familiar voice screaming. Aron's mother came running up the road behind them, yelling.

"Henry! Sir Gareth! Come quickly! They've taken the boys!"

Three

Aron stood in dazed disbelief in the center of the kitchen he'd grown up in, unable to process the idea this was real.

His mother wept at the table, obviously distraught and shaken; his older brother pulled a chair close and placed a comforting arm around her. Sir Gareth and his father spoke quietly in one corner next to the door, which still hung off its hinges from the attack. After a few moments, they turned and crossed over to the table. His father spoke more softly and hesitantly than Aron had ever heard him.

"Caroline," he almost whispered as he took the seat across from her and extended his hand over the table to take hers, "we need you to tell us everything."

His mother looked up, eyes rimmed in red, an ugly, blotchy bruise marring her cheek. She stared, uncomprehending, at his father and then up at Sir Gareth, who stood behind him.

"I've already told you," she said. "They took them. They busted down the door, and they took them."

"I know." His father squeezed her hand tighter, pain in his eyes. "But, please. Anything you can remember may help Sir Gareth find the boys."

His mom sniffled and took a deep breath, trying to calm herself as she began the tale again.

"I was at the counter, cutting potatoes for dinner," she began. "Caleb and Eli had just come in from their chores and were washing up when the alarm bells started to ring. They wanted to run out and see what was happening, but I made them stay here with me. I tried to convince them—and myself—that it was just another drill."

She paused, staring at the rough wood of the table for a moment, trying to compose herself. Then, she looked up again with determination and continued.

"The bells had barely stopped when something slammed into the door. At first, I thought maybe it was one of you coming home." She stared into the eyes of her husband and shuddered. "But then it came again and again. I told the boys to go to their room, and I grabbed the knife I'd been using to cut the potatoes. When the door broke, they rushed in, snarling and barking at each other. Five or six of them, at least. I cut the first one that came through, but the second one hit me with a club. I don't remember a whole lot after that. I was just lying on the floor. I couldn't move, only halfway seeing what was happening. I thought we were all dead."

Another pause, and tears began to flow again. Jonas squeezed his mother in a tight hug. Aron felt helpless. She had always been a rock in their family, and here she was, nearly unable to speak in her grief.

"I'm sorry," his father said again. "But we need to know every detail you can remember."

"They ran through the house. It was like I was here, but I wasn't. I could see them, but I couldn't move or make a noise. Several of them made a loud, howling sound, and they came running out of the boys' room. Caleb and Eli were trying to fight, but it didn't bother the goblins at all. I tried to get up, go after them, but I couldn't move. By the time I was able to pick myself up, they were long gone. That's when I came to get you."

Aron couldn't help but think about the rag doll he'd found on the goblin he killed in the mountains, and he shuddered. The thought of his brothers in the clutches of the creatures frightened him and put a sick lump in his stomach. He tried to comfort himself with the fact that Caleb was almost twelve. Maybe it would be OK. After all, Aron survived the mountains and a goblin when he was that age. But it had only been the one, and he didn't have to worry about a nine-year-old brother like Caleb would.

"Do you remember anything unusual about them?"

It was the first time the knight had spoken. His mother looked up at Gareth with a lost look on her face.

"They were goblins." Now, anger sparked in her eyes, replacing the grief. She snapped at the knight in a caustic voice that Aron had never heard from his mother, "They looked like goblins. Teeth, claws, and ugliness. They took my children, and you're standing here interrogating me instead of going after them."

Gareth had the decency to look embarrassed and inclined his head toward Aron's mother. "My apologies, ma'am. I meant no offense. It's just that anything you remember might help point us in the right direction."

Aron thought for a moment that his mother was going to explode in rage, but then her eyes widened, as if in realization. "Actually, two of them were dressed very strangely. I thought it was odd when I was lying there looking at them, but with everything happening…"

Gareth took a step forward, but Aron's father shook his head slightly, and the knight stepped back and waited.

"Go on," his Da said gently.

"Well, they were dressed better than the goblins we've seen before. They had on these sort of robes that looked new. It was almost like a uniform."

Gareth grunted, and Aron's father turned toward him with a quizzical expression. "What does it mean?"

"I don't know," the knight said honestly. "The

enemies we've captured tell Commander Kyle some strange stories. I need to get a message to him about this."

"We can't wait for Devan." Aron finally found his voice, and it burst forth with urgency. "We need to go after them now. Tonight."

Gareth gave him a hard glare. "Commander Kyle," he said stiffly, emphasizing the title, "needs to know. But you are correct. We will go after them tonight. Or, rather, I will. You will stay here with your family."

Aron couldn't have been more stunned if the knight had slapped him. He was Sir Gareth's squire, and these were his brothers.

"I can help," he said indignantly. "I can get Doubloon. He can track them down and destroy them."

"And when was the last time you saw the dragon?" Gareth asked.

Aron stared at the floor. "The day of the battle with the goblins."

"So, you intend to go into the mountains, unsure of whether or not you can find the dragon's home again, and not knowing if he's willing to help? It could take weeks to find him. Meanwhile, I can run them down tonight."

Aron thought again of the medallion hidden away in his trunk and started to speak up, but then Doubloon's words echoed in his head, "Keep it secret." He'd done that, even from his family. He paused, unsure what to do, but Sir Gareth saved him the decision.

"I believe your home was not targeted randomly," the knight said, stroking his chin as he considered.

"What do you mean?" Aron's father stood to stare at the knight.

"Every creature on the battlefield two years ago heard your son's name from the dragon's mouth. This was a coordinated attack. I thought the raid at the edge of the village was a weak effort, but now I believe it was a distraction. The true goal was your house."

Aron stared wide-eyed at his mentor, and his heart sank. Could Gareth be right? Could he be the reason his brothers had been kidnapped by monsters? The knight turned to him.

"That is why I don't want you on this hunt. For some reason, I believe they wanted you. They may even think they have you now. Whatever their purpose, I won't deliver you to them. I will find them, and I'll bring your brothers back this very night."

Sir Gareth straightened himself and turned to leave the house.

"I'm going, too," Aron's father said, crossing the room and grabbing the sword that leaned against the wall.

"Are you sure, Henry?" The knight cast a glance at Aron's mother. "Your family needs you."

"Jonas and Aron can take care of things here.

Those monsters have my other boys, and they need me more."

Gareth nodded and turned again toward the door.

"Henry?" Both men turned to look at his mother. "Bring them back safe."

Aron's father looked grim, but Sir Gareth drew his sword and saluted her. "I swear to you that not a hair on their heads will be harmed."

Aron hoped his master could keep that promise.

He felt almost relaxed when the time came to herd the sheep
back to their pen for the night.

He felt almost relaxed when the time came to herd the sheep
back to their pen for the night.

Four

The night passed, and the next morning came and went. Still, there was no sign of Sir Gareth, Aron's father, or his brothers. When Jonas returned mid-morning, Aron had not slept. He'd spent the night sitting at the table with his mother, who remained distraught. He worried about her. She hadn't spoken much through the night. She just sat and stared, sobbing occasionally. Aron would hug her or grip her hand, and she would return the gesture weakly.

"I should have stopped them," she repeated on occasion. Every time, Aron pulled her close and told her there was nothing more she could have done. It was true. He thought back to the terror he felt when facing one goblin, and his mother had been trying to fend off five or six.

Jonas's wife Nelly came with him, and she took

Aron's place at the table, comforting his mother as he went with his older brother to take care of the chores on the farm. He didn't want to leave, but Jonas was insistent.

"The animals still have to be fed, and the work still needs to be done. When Da comes back, I don't want to be the one who has to face him and tell him we shirked our duties. I don't think you want that, either."

The two shared a half-hearted laugh, but a shadow hung over them. They both remembered Sir Gareth's promise to their mother that he'd return with their younger brothers before morning. They both knew their father should be back by now and that something wasn't right. Neither of them wanted to give voice to that thought.

Ironically, Aron found his time in the pasture with the sheep that afternoon almost soothing. He remembered the last time he'd been there, his father's disappointment in his daydreams, and the events that eventually led to his running away over the mountains in a childish attempt to become a knight. In a way, he regretted the things that had happened that day and felt a little silly about his actions, but he knew he would do it all again for what he gained.

No imaginary dragons swooped down on the field for Aron to fight in his daydreams. Now that he knew a real one, he also knew that his naïve ideas about dragons, knights, and the world in general were mostly wrong. His parents told him repeatedly how much he'd grown during his time away and with Sir Gareth and how proud they were of him. He supposed that was true. He certainly had a different perspective on things. With most of his time spent training as a squire, he now found a certain satisfaction in the mundane tasks of the farm that he'd so hated back then.

He felt almost relaxed when the time came to herd the sheep back to their pen for the night. He imagined that his Da and brothers would be waiting for him around the table when he arrived. He knew it was a vain hope, but he let it warm him as he headed home.

NELLY HELD her finger to her lips as he entered the house, shushing him. She pointed toward his parents' room, and he tiptoed over to glance in. His mother slept soundly on the bed. That, at least, was good. Aron's own exhaustion caught up with him as he watched her, and he felt a weight settle on his shoulders.

"You should get some rest, too, once we get some food in you." Jonas placed an arm around his younger brother as he whispered to him. Aron hadn't heard him come in or felt him approach. He nodded mutely as Jonas led him over to the table and sat him down.

Nelly had prepared a meal for them—the potatoes his mother had been cutting the night before with some pork cutlets. It wasn't quite as tasty as his mother's meal would have been, but Aron barely tasted it anyway. No one spoke as the three finished their dinner. They all knew something was very wrong.

When he was done, Aron rinsed his plate in the washbasin and walked wordlessly to his room. He collapsed on the cot and was asleep almost as soon as his head landed.

THE NEXT FEW days passed in much the same way. Aron's mother returned a bit more to her normal self. At least, she was up and moving around, tending to her usual chores. She remained distant and quiet. Nelly stayed around the house during the day to help her and keep her company while Aron and Jonas took care of the farm.

Aron tried to lose himself in the chores, focusing on what needed to be done, rather than the worries that were weighing on his mind. Even mucking the pigsty and dodging King Alfred was better than thinking about what might have happened to the missing members of their household. Those thoughts haunted the nights, when he lay awake on his cot waiting for exhaustion to take them away.

Meals were eaten largely in silence, and he and his mother retired to their rooms almost immediately after, with Jonas and Nelly heading back to their own home.

He wondered if it would be like this forever. He couldn't let that happen. He had to do something.

ON THE MORNING of the fifth day after his father and Sir Gareth had set out to rescue his brothers, Aron emerged from his room prepared not for the day's chores, but for a journey. He'd filled his pack with all the things he would need. He'd learned his lessons from his time spent in the mountains without necessities like flint and tinder. Doubloon's amulet was tucked deep inside, wrapped in his extra clothes.

Aron strapped on his belt, sword on one side and the fine skinning knife Devan had given him on the other, and he threw his cloak over his shoulders. He'd looked longingly at the armor he'd been issued but decided to leave it in the chest. It would only slow him down, and if all went to plan, he wouldn't need to fight anything face-to-face.

When he entered the kitchen, his mother stared at him for a moment, then stood, her face twisting into a rare look of anger.

"What do you think you're doing, young man?"

Jonas rose and tried to place a hand on her shoulder, but she brushed it away.

"I'm going to bring them home." Aron pulled himself up to his full height, almost even with his mother now.

"You will do no such thing. Now, take that off and go help your brother with the chores. I won't hear any more of this nonsense."

Aron didn't want to argue with his mother. She'd been through enough. But he had to do this. He was the only one who could.

"I will not." It hurt his heart to speak to his mother so, but he felt like he had no choice. "I'm going to find Doubloon. He'll help. We'll bring them home."

His mother's face went white. Her expression scared him. He'd never seen such rage in her features. Aron wanted to slink back into his room, pack everything back in the chest, and go tend the sheep. He couldn't. He steeled himself and stood his ground as she crossed the small room toward him. He braced, thinking she might strike him for the first time in his life. Instead, she stopped, nearly nose-to-nose with him, and stared into his eyes. It broke him.

"Please, Mum. I need to do this. We can save them. I know we can. You've seen what Doubloon can do. No goblins are going to stop him. We'll find them, and we'll bring them home."

Her anger abated, and her eyes watered with tears that she tried to hold back.

"I can't lose anyone else."

"You won't. Doubloon will take care of me...and everyone else."

She pulled him into a crushing hug, letting the tears flow freely. He tried to fight back his own, but he couldn't. They made hot trails down his cheeks as he returned the embrace. Finally, she pulled away, gripping him by the shoulders and looking into his eyes again.

"How will you find the dragon?"

"I just need to get close. He'll know I'm there. That's what happened last time."

"You will not go alone," she said sternly. "Go and fetch one of the other knights. Have him travel with you."

"I will," Aron said stiffly. He hated lying to his mother, but he had no intention of taking anyone else with him. He wouldn't betray the secret of the amulet that Doubloon had trusted to him. He didn't know why the dragon had been so insistent about not revealing it, but he knew there had to be a good reason.

"Promise me," his mother continued, "that you will let the dragon do the fighting. I want you back, too."

"I promise." He meant that one. He knew he was no knight, at least not yet. Gareth had made that clear. He wasn't about to take on an army of goblins.

She gave him another long hug, then backed away, wiping her eyes with the corner of her apron.

"Go and bring them home."

Nervousness and anticipation swirled within him as Aron walked up the road toward the mountain. This time, he walked the path in full daylight with the knowledge and blessing of his mother…well, sort of. She did think he was taking one of the knights with him. He regretted that fib, but he wanted to move quickly. There was no real rebellion in this trip, as there had been two years ago when he'd run away, but he still felt the same sort of nervous excitement. He longed to see Doubloon again, to fly with him, but the reason for their reunion still weighed heavily.

He also couldn't shake a nagging question in the back of his mind. Would the dragon even come? They'd had no contact for nearly two years, even though Aron had tried to reach out through the mental link they'd often used to talk to each other. Maybe that had been some trick of Doubloon's magic that he'd removed when he left. Or maybe they were simply too far apart for it to work. *Or maybe*, the doubting part of himself whispered in his ear, *he doesn't want anything to do with you.*

Aron wouldn't listen to that. He couldn't. Doubloon was his friend. He would come. He had to come.

He tried to remain upbeat as he walked the road out of the village, but doubt had settled into his mind. What if the dragon didn't come? What would he do then? He couldn't go after his family on his own. He had no idea where they might be, and if his Da and Sir Gareth couldn't handle whatever they'd run into, what hope did he have? He remembered the knight besting him in seconds just a few days ago. Anything that could beat Gareth would handle Aron in no time.

If Doubloon didn't come, he'd just have to continue over the mountain, back to Lanfield, though he was reluctant to return to the city after his last experience there. He'd go to Devan—Commander Kyle, that's how he had to think of the man now, Aron reminded himself. He would know what to do. He could help.

Aron walked briskly and didn't take note of much along the way. He never paused or slowed until he found himself in the shadow of the mountain. Before the road began to rise, he stopped, considering how to proceed. He was far enough from the village now that the dragon should be able to meet him without drawing too much attention. That is, if the goblins hadn't left spies to watch him. Aron considered that possibility for the first time as he remembered Sir Gareth's suspicions that the kidnapping had something to do with his relationship with Doubloon.

Well, if there were spies here, they'd just have to handle them. Aron left the road then, walking into an open meadow that was screened from the village by a grove of trees. He sat cross-legged on the ground and opened his pack, digging around until his fingers found the cold metal of the amulet Doubloon had given him. He drew it from the bag and sat for a moment, holding it before him. He met the eyes of the dragon that was stamped on it, gold like his friend, but much colder. He turned it over and looked at what he'd first taken for a red jewel. He'd later learned that it was the ruby scale of his friend's father, encased in the gold and peeking out.

Aron realized he didn't know what he was supposed to do with the amulet. Doubloon didn't really explain that part very well. He searched his memory trying to remember what his friend told him in those final moments together.

"Should you ever need me, all you need to do is call." He was almost certain that's what the dragon had said.

He pulled the amulet to his chest, gripping it tightly, and closed his eyes.

"Doubloon, if you can hear me, please come," he whispered. "I need you. My family needs you."

He repeated it a few times, fixing the image of his friend in his mind. He didn't know if that would help, but it couldn't hurt. After a few minutes, he opened his eyes again, half expecting to see the dragon there, as if transported by some sort of magic. He was disappointed. It was a silly thought, Aron knew. Doubloon must be far away, but he'd hoped there was some sort of extraordinary power in the trinket that would make his friend appear out of thin air.

With a sigh, Aron wrapped the amulet in his clothes again and tucked it back into the pack. He pulled himself to his feet, slinging it over one shoulder, and headed back to the edge of the meadow. He sat down beneath a large oak tree, leaning against the rough trunk. He opened the pack again and dug out one of the apples he'd stocked for the journey. As he crunched into it, he remembered the sweet fruit from the merchant outside of Lanfield that he'd used one of his last pennies to buy. The ones that grew in his village weren't quite that tasty, but they were still good, and it would fill his belly, which had started to complain that he hadn't eaten breakfast that morning.

He stared at the skies as he ate, searching for the familiar shadow, willing it to appear. Nothing. He needed to be patient, he reminded himself. He'd give the dragon a few hours, and if there was still no sign of his friend, he would try the amulet again. The doubts began to creep back into his head. What if he'd used the magic wrong? What if Doubloon just didn't want to see him?

He centered himself and tried to push them away using the meditation techniques that Gareth had taught him, even though he hated them. He had to give his friend every chance to come, had to be patient, fight the frustration that haunted him. There was nothing to do but wait, and it could be a very long wait.

Six

The goblins fled ahead of Aron, scattering across the open plain of the battlefield. He felt the powerful muscles of the dragon move beneath him, then heat blasted him in the face as Doubloon unleashed another gout of deadly fire into the enemy. As it struck, the last of the ranks of monsters and men broke and ran. The knights and townspeople below raised their swords in the air and gave a great cheer. Aron pumped his fist above his head and released a cry of victory as well, but it was short-lived.

In the distance, the sky darkened, as if a storm had suddenly formed on the horizon. The very air and earth around them seemed to rumble and shake. Their allies on the ground fell silent, cowering back from this new evil.

"What is it?" Aron asked, but his friend didn't answer immediately.

They flew ever closer to the boiling, black clouds. Lightning rolled within the ominous darkness, and thunder rumbled. He didn't know what lurked behind, but he knew it wasn't good. A cold fear filled him, a dread he couldn't quite explain. Something evil was coming, invading every fiber of his being.

"There are dangers here," Doubloon said, breaking the silence.

Something nudged at Aron. He rolled over and mumbled, his eyes cracking open. A shadow fell over him, and he woke with a start, heart racing in panic. He rolled instinctively to the side, scrambling to get his sword out of the scabbard.

"You really shouldn't sleep out in the open like that, youngling." Doubloon repeated, "There are dangers here. If I can sneak up on you, just imagine what a goblin could do."

Aron snapped back to himself at the sound of his friend's voice. Relief flooded him. The last few days really must have caught up with him. He couldn't believe he'd fallen asleep while waiting on the dragon. The dragon! Doubloon was here. He sprang to his feet and ran to his old friend, wrapping his arms as far around the beast's neck as they would go in a tight hug. They went much farther than the last time they'd met.

"Doubloon," he shouted. "You came!"

"Of course." The dragon reached one of his great

front legs gently around Aron's shoulders, awkwardly attempting to return the hug.

"I wasn't sure." The boy pulled back to look at his friend, tears streaming down his face.

Doubloon gave him a stern look and *harrumph*ed. "You should know a dragon—a friend—always keeps his word. Why ever would you think I wouldn't come?"

Aron stared up into the dragon's offended expression, then a huge smile broke through the tears. Doubloon chuckled as well.

"I've missed you so much," Aron said.

"I've missed you, too, little one. Only, you're not nearly as little as you were."

"Where have you been? I tried calling to you several times, but you didn't answer."

"Here and there," the dragon said. "You and your people made me curious, so I've traveled up and down the mountain range, observing. From a safe distance, of course. What of you? Are you a knight yet?"

Aron looked a bit frustrated and averted his eyes toward the ground. "No."

"What's wrong? Are things not going well?"

"Gareth says I lack the discipline of a knight. I'm trying, but it's hard…"

Doubloon laughed. "Discipline, you say? I can't imagine why you might be having a hard time with that."

Aron jerked his head up in annoyance, but then he saw the mirth in the dragon's gaze, and he couldn't help but smile as well. Then, the boy's eyes widened in panic as he remembered his purpose.

"We don't have time," he said in a rush. "We have to move. We have to save my brothers...and my Da...and Sir Gareth."

"Slow down, youngling. What's happened? Tell me the story."

Aron took a few deep breaths to calm himself and started from the beginning. He told the dragon of the goblin raid and how it seemed like a ruse to distract from the real mission—to kidnap his brothers.

"Sir Gareth thinks they may have come for me and gotten my brothers instead. He thinks it may have something to do with you, with how you shouted my name over the battlefield. He and Da went after them, said they'd be back before nightfall. That was a week ago, and we've neither seen nor heard from them since. They're in trouble. I know it. We need to go after them. We have to save them."

The dragon looked thoughtful. "It pains me to think that I may have somehow brought this grief upon you."

Doubloon backed away and lowered his head to stare into the eyes of his young friend. "Know this. I will fix it. We will save them. All of them."

Aron nodded through tears. Looking into the dragon's eyes, things suddenly didn't seem as hopeless as they had a few minutes before. What were a bunch of goblins to his friend, who had single-handedly defeated an army of the vile creatures? Aron wiped his eyes on his sleeve and stood a little taller, the power of Doubloon lending him confidence.

The dragon lowered his wing for the boy to climb aboard. Aron noticed with surprise that the harness they had built was already in place, and he clambered into it, fastening himself down.

"Now," Doubloon said. "Tell me which way they traveled. We have goblins to hunt."

With that, the dragon bunched his muscles and launched them into the skies.

Seven

For two days, Aron and Doubloon traveled mostly by night, so the dragon felt comfortable ranging farther afield in an attempt to locate the goblins. Aron at first expressed concern that they might miss them in the darkness, but Doubloon assured him that a dragon's night vision was far better than a human's.

"Do you see the three deer in that meadow below us?" the dragon asked.

Aron leaned over and peered down at the ground below, but he could barely make out the vague shapes of treetops. He wasn't convinced.

"You know I can't see anything in the dark. How do I know you're not just making that up?"

Doubloon chuckled at his companion's obstinance and dove, swooping low above the clearing. As the tops of the trees nearly brushed the dragon's legs, he issued a quick burst of flame from his throat, lighting up the meadow below. Illuminated by the fireball, three white tails bounced away from them and back into the forest.

"Now do you believe me?"

Aron huffed and sat back in the harness, a sulking frown on his face.

"Aside from that, the goblins will likely have fires that make them easy for even your weak human eyes to see."

The boy knew that his friend was joking with him, but he was in no mood for it. He'd expected them to catch up with the goblins right away and already be back home. He knew the monsters would be no challenge for the dragon, and they'd once again be heroes. It would be a clear sign that he was ready for the knighthood, despite what Gareth said or thought.

Instead, they'd searched for two nights without the slightest sign of goblins or his family. Aron didn't even know if they were headed in the right direction. He knew only which way Gareth and his father had pursued them. The goblins could have taken a completely different turn, and he and Doubloon could be flying further and further from their goal without even knowing it. Bigger worries than that gnawed at his gut as well. It had been more than a week since his brothers had been stolen and his Da and the knight had followed. Goblins weren't known for taking prisoners. There was a strong chance that even if they did find the monsters, they wouldn't find his brothers or his father.

Aron pushed those thoughts out of his mind. He couldn't let himself believe that. They would find them, and Doubloon would rescue them.

As if sensing his unease, the dragon spoke to him in a calm and soothing voice.

"I know you worry, youngling, but do not. We will find them and bring them home."

"How can you be so sure? We don't even know if we're going the right way…and they're goblins."

"Normally, I would agree. But there is something odd about this entire situation. Goblins do not take prisoners. I suspect your knight was correct. There was a reason they wanted your brothers, and I believe that makes them safe…for a time, at least."

Aron didn't like the sound of those last words. He appreciated that the dragon wanted to make him feel better, but often, Doubloon could be a little blunt. He lacked the human concept of empathy and would speak the truth, even when it might not be the best approach.

They flew in silence for a time. As much as Aron had longed to be back in the skies with his friend throughout the years they'd been apart, he found that he couldn't enjoy it as he should. Flying mostly at night took much of the wonder out of riding dragonback, and even when the sun rose on their flights in the mornings, he still couldn't muster much excitement. Their mission weighed on him.

Aron leaned back in the harness and gazed at the stars overhead. He tried to pick out the constellations his father had attempted to teach him, but he'd never had much of a head for it. His lack of attention to the subject frustrated his Da. He'd scolded the boy, pointing out that he needed to know these things, so he could find his way home if he were ever lost at night. Back then, Aron couldn't have imagined being far enough from home to need such a skill. He laughed bitterly at that thought now.

"Something wrong?" Doubloon asked on hearing the unusual sound from his friend.

"No. Just remembering something."

"Would you like to talk about it?"

"Not particularly."

The dragon bobbed his head slightly. "If you do, you have only to speak it."

Aron resumed his study of the stars, though he saw little in them but specks of distant light. That wasn't exactly true, though. There, nearly directly overhead, he thought he spotted a cluster he remembered from the book his father had shown him—the Magician. A triangle of stars with a brighter one above and to the right, shining like a jewel atop a staff. He struggled to remember what his Da's lessons had taught about the Magician and his position in the sky, but he couldn't.

They could definitely use a magician right now, if

such a thing existed. Perhaps he could cast some sort of spell that would show them the way. Da would have said he was being silly. Magic users were just myths, after all. Then again, so were dragons.

His attention came back to the here and now as Doubloon slowed his flight to a near stop, hovering in the night sky. Aron sat up and looked around but, as usual, could see nothing in the gloom.

"What is it?" he asked his friend.

"I am not sure," the dragon answered. "I believe I see the light of fires ahead—many fires."

Aron squinted in the direction his friend was looking, but he saw nothing. "Do you think it's them?"

"Doubtful. There are far too many for a small band of goblins. It looks like a large gathering, maybe a town or a village. We should at least investigate, though. They are still miles away, but we should reach them by morning."

Butterflies bounced in Aron's stomach as thoughts about what lay ahead whirled through his head. Could they have found them at last? Or had they discovered something else even more dangerous? Aron thought about his dreams of the darkness on the horizon and had a frightening idea.

"What if it's not a town? What if it's an army?" he asked.

"Hmm." Doubloon pondered a moment. "I suppose it's possible. The fires do seem somewhat uniform."

The thought troubled Aron. If it were an army, what would the two of them do alone? Well, the dragon had fought and defeated an army of goblins before. Aron had no doubt he could do it again.

"Calm yourself, youngling, and rest," his friend said, sensing Aron's turmoil. "We shall see what awaits us soon enough."

He tried to take the dragon's advice and leaned back. He even tried one of Gareth's dumb meditation exercises in an attempt to tamp down his excitement, but they were even more useless on the back of a dragon than in that little hut in the village.

Finally, he gave up and leaned forward, peering into the darkness, hoping to spot what his friend could already see. There was nothing he could do but wait.

What they could see from their perch
looked more like a small city that had
been hastily built on the plain below
the mountains.

Eight

ron and Doubloon sat atop a rocky outcrop as the sun rose, slowly revealing the enemy encampment in the distance. Aron could take no pleasure in the fact that he'd been right. They had expected to find a tiny band of goblins, but what they could see from their perch looked more like a small city that had been hastily built on the plain below the mountains. He squinted to make out the details the dragon could see clearly.

On the northern end of the camp sat row upon row of what appeared to be modest white tents in the familiar triangular shape of the simple ones the people in his village sometimes used when they traveled. Beyond them lay a much less orderly group of shelters. Unlike the perfect alignment of the white tents, these were arranged in a haphazard manner with seemingly no rhyme or reason. No one was quite like any other.

They came in all shapes, and garish colors stood out here and there amongst the mostly brown, gray, and green that surrounded them.

The tents on the eastern end of the encampment, framed by the rising sun, were the ones that caught Aron's attention. There were three of them, much larger than the rest, with the one at the center appearing to dwarf his home back in the village. From what he could see, it looked like the kind of setup that might be used to house a king in the field. Doubloon confirmed his suspicions.

"That big one will be where we find their leader. It's much finer than the others, made of expensive fabrics."

"Do you see any sign of my brothers or Da or Sir Gareth?"

"No," Doubloon answered. "All of the humans that I can see appear to be soldiers of some sort. Most are only now coming out of their tents. They are in the white ones. The others belong to goblins. I cannot tell how many of those there are, but there are many."

"Not more than you fought back in the village, though?"

"No. Not nearly as many, in fact, but if your father and brothers are down there, I can hardly burn everything down, can I?"

Aron's eyes widened at the realization, and the dragon's mouth twitched upward on one side. "Do not worry, little one. If we are in the right place, we will figure out the best way to keep them safe. If we are not, your knights should still know about this. It could be a threat to them."

The boy yawned and leaned back against Doubloon's leg. Despite the dragon's urging, he had not been able to sleep. He was torn between exhaustion and frustration. He strained his eyes, hoping to catch a glimpse of a familiar shape, but the figures that were beginning to bustle around the camp looked like little more than ants from this distance. He couldn't even tell the humans from the goblins.

They sat and watched as the sun rose higher in the sky, but still, Doubloon had seen no sign of prisoners. He described what would be everyday activities in an army camp. They cooked their breakfast over fires, some began doing chores, others moved to an open area in the center of the camp where they practiced military drills. A small group of men, who Doubloon said appeared to be officers of some sort, had come out of one of the larger tents, but no one had emerged from the other two.

"We should both rest," the dragon said at last. "I'm afraid the goblins we search for are not among these. I see no sign of prisoners anywhere. I do not believe they are here."

That could mean many things, Aron knew. It could be that he and Doubloon were off track and stumbled upon the army by accident. He didn't want to consider the other possibility—that the goblins they searched for were here, but his family was not—but he couldn't keep it out of his head. He slumped against his friend, and the dragon stretched his neck down, nudging the boy gently in an awkward attempt to comfort him.

"Do not worry, youngling. We will find them. I feel it in my bones."

The confidence in the dragon's voice made Aron feel a little better, but he couldn't keep those dark thoughts from invading. Doubloon shifted, curling his body around his small friend protectively.

"You should sleep now," he said softly, or at least as softly as a deep, gravelly dragon voice could. "You will feel better when you are rested."

To Aron's surprise, Doubloon began to hum, something the boy hadn't known he could do. It was an unfamiliar tune, but somehow quite soothing. After a few minutes, a weight seemed to lift from Aron's soul, and despite his struggles to keep an eye on the encampment below, he felt himself begin to drift away.

His eyes drooped. Just as he was about to doze off, the weight of all that worry and anxiety slammed back down on top of him. Doubloon's humming had stopped suddenly, jarring him out of what he realized had been some sort of magic on the dragon's part. His friend raised his head and stared back down toward the army. Aron could feel the tension thrumming through the dragon's body.

"What is it?"

Doubloon didn't answer right away. "Something

strange. One of the large tents, the smallest of the three, just opened. A group of goblins emerged, but they are different. They seem to be wearing some sort of uniform. I've never seen such a thing."

"What does it look like?"

"Black, almost like robes. Many of them have hoods pulled over their heads."

Aron sat straight up, now wide awake. "The goblins that took Caleb and Eli were wearing those. Mum described them. Everyone thought it was strange."

Then a low rumble began in the dragon's throat. He pulled himself out of his protective posture and stood—an aggressive stance.

"What's happening?"

"The goblins surround a small group of humans. They seem to be leading them out into the field. Two of them are quite small—smaller than you."

"Caleb and Eli?" Aron squinted and peered out across the camp, trying to make out any details, but it was useless. His eyes were not nearly as sharp as the dragon's.

"Perhaps, but I do not know. I would not recognize your brothers."

Aron was up now and clambering to get back in the harness. "You have to get me closer. I need to see."

"Calm yourself, youngling. Do you not remember? There is a better way." Doubloon spoke a word in the sinuous language of the dragons, and a familiar queasiness settled in the boy's stomach as his vision swam.

Then, he recalled the flight over the battlefield and knew what was happening.

He closed his eyes for a moment, and when he opened them again, it seemed as if he was standing in the camp. His vision blurred a bit at the edges, but he could see the details much more clearly. His eyes darted to the larger tents on the eastern end, and he saw the group of strangely dressed goblins marching out into an open field. He spotted the prisoners shuffling along uncomfortably in the middle of the group. His Da and Sir Gareth marched resolutely, backs straight and heads held high. Caleb and Eli crowded close to the two adults, glancing around nervously. The fear in their eyes sent an arrow straight through Aron's heart, but then it soared, the pain replaced by joy. He and Doubloon had found them, and they were alive.

"It's them!" he shouted. "They're alive! We have to go get them."

"Settle yourself." The calm in the dragon's voice was maddening to Aron. Didn't he understand? His family was in danger. They needed to get down there right away to save them.

"We need to go now!" he yelled.

"Not yet. Look again and think. They could have kept them inside the tent, but they are marching them around out in the open. There can be only one reason for that. They want them to be seen. We should rest, wait for the cover of darkness. Then, we can come on them unawares."

"We don't have time to wait. We don't know what they're going to do with them. They may not have until dark."

"If they were going to harm them, they would have done so already. We are expected. It is a trap."

"What can they do to trap a dragon? You defeated their whole army. There's nothing they can do to you."

"Likely not, but we should still use caution. There is no reason to rush into what we know to be a ruse."

Doubloon reached down and nudged him again, comfortingly. "Let's get some rest. After dark, I will go and get them."

Aron pulled away from the dragon and met his eyes. Hot tears traced trails down Aron's face. They were so close, and now the creature he'd thought was his friend refused to go and save his family. His features twisted, and he wanted to lash out with all of his anger. Instead, something inside him broke. He fell to his knees and sobbed.

He looked up to the dragon through red, bleary eyes and said one word.

"Please."

Doubloon stared into those eyes for a moment, then gave a resigned sigh.

"As you wish."

The dragon bunched his muscles and launched himself into the sky. He came screaming down out of the mountains onto the camp below. Aron leaped to his feet and ran to the edge of the rocks to watch the rescue. Chaos descended on the humans and goblins as they spotted the dragon racing toward them. Without Doubloon's magical sight, they looked like ants scrambling out of a kicked hill.

He kept an eye on the area where he knew his family and Sir Gareth were as the dragon approached on his attack route. That's when he noticed someone finally emerge from the largest of the tents. He couldn't make out any details, of course, but the figure stood alone and seemed to be the only one not panicking. The newcomer raised his hands.

Aron's eyes darted back to Doubloon, coming in hard, and a moment of doubt seized him. Maybe the dragon had been right. As his friend swooped across the open area of the camp, a great net shot up from the ground in front of him. Aron's breath caught in his throat, but then he realized how silly it was. They thought they could catch a dragon with a net? He would burn right through. As if on cue, a great blast of flame erupted from his friend's throat, engulfing the would-be trap. When it faded, Aron's eyes widened. The net still stood. Doubloon could not stop. He slammed into it, getting entangled, and fell hard to the ground below with an earth-shaking thud.

Aron winced, but he still wasn't worried. He didn't know why the net hadn't burned, but Doubloon would rip the thing to shreds and be right back in the air. Then, he'd be angry. He watched as the dragon struggled to free himself, but he only seemed to be getting more entangled. The boy panicked, realizing he'd led his friend right into the trap the dragon had warned him about.

"Doubloon!" he yelled. Then, he stopped himself. The dragon wouldn't be able to hear him from this distance. Instead, he reached out with his mind.

Doubloon! Doubloon!

There was no answer.

Nine

It had taken Aron the rest of that day and most of the next to bring himself within easy sight of the camp where Doubloon and his family were being held captive. Every muscle in his body ached. His hands burned with cuts and scrapes he'd sustained climbing rocks.

When he and the dragon had chosen their perch to spy on the enemy, they hadn't considered that Aron might have to get down on his own. He'd clung to the sheer stone drop in terror as he'd descended, his desire to be on solid ground as quickly as possible warring with the knowledge that he had to be slow and deliberate in his movements, or else he might reach the ground much more quickly than was survivable. He had never breathed a bigger sigh of relief than when he was finally on a relatively level surface below the outcropping.

He had to climb a few more times along the way, but none as harrowing as that first one. They also hadn't considered paths for getting down the mountain. After all, Doubloon could fly. Aron used whatever trails and openings he could find, keeping an eye on the sun to make sure he was moving generally to the east, where the camp lay.

That night, he slept fitfully, hidden behind the cover of some scrub brush. He'd been more prepared this time than his previous trip into the mountains, but it didn't help as much as it might have. While he had the tools to build a fire, he dared not. He feared being spotted from the camp below, and he also had no idea if the army might be sending patrols into the mountains. So, it had been a cold, dark night with some dried meat and his one remaining apple for dinner.

Aron was lower now, almost on the level of the camp, but still high enough to survey what was happening. He crouched behind bushes, peering through to take in the scene. For much of his journey, he hadn't been able to see what was going on, and he'd been worried that they may have done something to Doubloon. From here, though, he could see that the dragon was still in the area where he'd fallen, still wrapped up tightly. It appeared the net had been spread a little and fastened to the ground. His friend was no longer quite as twisted inside it, but it still didn't look very comfortable. He was, at least, alive and mostly unharmed. He hoped the same was still true of his family and Gareth.

Anger burned in Aron's chest, but it mingled with the guilt of the knowledge that this situation was at least partially his doing. If he'd listened to Doubloon and waited until dark, the army may have never seen the attack coming. The dragon might have struck a devastating blow and freed his family. Even now, they could be on their way back to the village. But he'd let emotions and fears overcome him, the very things Gareth often told him that he could not give in to. He'd convinced his friend to abandon caution and charge into battle. Now, his best chance to rescue his Da and his brothers was also a prisoner, and Aron had no idea how he could fix this alone.

Doubloon. He reached out with his mind again, as he'd done several times over the last day, hoping against hope that the dragon would hear him and respond. Just like every other time, his plea was met with silence. Something was very wrong, and Aron had no idea what it was.

The rage that bubbled inside him demanded that he draw his sword, charge down into the camp, and cut his friend free. But he knew that would be a stupid course of action. There were hundreds of goblins and human warriors down there—enough to capture not only Sir Gareth, but also a dragon. The only thing he could do by charging in would be put himself in chains next to everyone else. He had to be smarter than that, but he had no idea what that meant.

He watched in the fading light until the fires began to blaze up, and soon, it was too dark for him to see much. He thought about using the cover of night to sneak into the camp, but there would almost certainly be patrols this close. He considered how he'd rushed Doubloon and how that had turned out. No, he needed more information before he could decide what to do.

With a sigh, Aron settled back against a tree and rummaged in his pack for the meat strips that were the only food he had left. At least he had plenty of those. He ripped a chunk off with his teeth and chewed on it as he contemplated. He wondered what Sir Gareth or Commander Kyle would do. He knew right away that they would get help, but that wasn't an option for him. Even if he could find his way back to the village or to Lanfield from here, it would take days, if not weeks, to get there on foot. By then, his friends and family could be dead and the army nowhere to be found. This was up to him.

He barely slept that night, on edge from being so close to the camp with the understanding that he was in very real danger of being discovered and taken prisoner as well. Every little sound in the darkness made him clutch his sword, eyes darting back and forth, trying to see where it came from.

The sun peeking over the eastern horizon brought

a bit of relief. At least he'd be able to see a threat coming, even if he was in no condition to deal with it.

As the camp below began to wake for the day, he crept back up to the bushes, trying to make himself as comfortable as possible. He lay on his stomach, eyes scanning for any information he could use to form a plan. As the morning wore on, there wasn't much. The only creatures that approached Doubloon were the goblins in the strange black robes. In the morning and again around noon, a small group of them tossed chunks of meat toward his mouth from a safe distance away. The net had enough give that his friend was able to gulp them down. On occasion, a single goblin would approach him, getting a bit closer. It appeared to be trying to speak with him, which was silly. Goblins were monsters. They didn't talk. Still, he wondered if Doubloon could communicate with them somehow, maybe mind-to-mind like he did with Aron.

He longed to see his family and Sir Gareth come out of that tent again, needed to confirm that they were still all right. But they didn't. Doubloon was correct all along. It had been a trap, and now that it had snapped shut, they no longer needed the bait.

Aron made note of all the guard posts around the camp, and it seemed they had a small patrol of human warriors walking the perimeter at all times. The odd, black-robed goblins, however, seemed to be able to come and go freely. He saw several leave the camp during the course of the morning and early afternoon.

The human guards gave them a wide berth. He knew that might be good knowledge to have, but his mind was fuzzy from lack of rest, and he couldn't quite connect the dots. He'd been lying as still and quietly as possible all day, and his limbs had gone stiff and painful. He rolled onto his back and stretched, his eyelids drooping. Well, he'd rest them for a moment, and then back to his watch. He needed to come up with some sort of plan. He had to get down to the camp. Had to…

A STRANGE SOUND awoke Aron with a start. As he cracked his eyelids, he was dismayed to see that the sky had begun to darken. He'd been asleep for hours. How had he let that happen? The sound came again, a grunt to his right. In a panic, he rolled to the left and heard something thump against the ground where he'd been lying a moment before.

He came to his feet, running on instinct and Gareth's training more than anything else. He found himself staring into the twisted features of one of the black-robed goblins. Its hood was thrown back, and it looked much like any of the other creatures he'd seen. Its mouth contorted into a snarl, showing sharp, jagged teeth below a bulbous nose. The skin was a blotchy brown and green; its yellow eyes glared at him with hatred, and it raised the club intended to break Aron's bones high above its head for another strike. The boy's sword was out then, and he flowed right into his training, blocking the strike and taking a chunk out of the heavy stick.

The goblin growled and swung again wildly, leaving Aron no time to think. He acted on instinct alone, trying to anticipate where the club would come from next, darting his sword left and right to parry the attacks. The creature in front of him was difficult to predict, though. It fought with no discipline, a mad rage in its eyes as it made frenzied, jerky strikes with its weapon. After a few successful blocks that each gouged another piece of wood out of the roughly carved club, one of the goblin's attacks finally got through. Aron managed to twist, catching the blow on his shoulder instead of the side of the head, as the monster had intended. That would have ended the fight and likely his life.

The hit he'd taken was bad enough. After the initial pain of the blow, his left arm went numb and felt useless and limp at his side. Tears leaked from his eyes, and the goblin grinned. That made Aron angry, and he launched his own series of chaotic attacks with his sword. That shifted the battle, causing his opponent to backpedal as the blade chopped away at its crude club. When they broke apart, the goblin scrambled backward out of his reach and stared, dumbfounded, at its weapon, which now looked like a branch that had been hacked at with a hatchet.

Aron began to circle, blade at the ready, looking for the opportunity to strike. The goblin moved with him, keeping a wary eye out and staring at its weakened club as if not quite sure what to do. Then, it seemed to have an idea. Sweeping an arm out, the creature slapped the end of the stick against a nearby tree. With a sharp crack, the part above the sword strikes broke off, leaving a jagged, sharp point at the end. The goblin snarled and charged, its improvised spear aimed straight at the boy's chest.

Aron danced backward, avoiding the blow, but the monster's attack left it off-balance. He sprung on the opening, sword arcing toward the creature's head. It managed to get what was left of the club up in the way of the blade, knocking the attack off target slightly. The sword struck the goblin's temple with the flat, rather than the edge. It was enough, though. The monster went limp and dropped immediately to the ground, unconscious.

Aron stood over the goblin and raised his blade to strike the killing blow, but he hesitated. He knew the monster wouldn't have, but knights were supposed to be better, right? It seemed dishonorable to strike down a helpless opponent, even if it was a goblin. He could imagine the earful that Gareth would give him if he were here right now, but Aron couldn't bring himself to do it.

With a sigh, he sheathed his sword and tested his injured arm. He was able to raise it, and he didn't think it was broken. It tingled with pins and needles, but the feeling was beginning to return. He rummaged through his pack, pulling out a length of rope. He tied the goblin's hands and feet, then cut a piece off its own filthy garments to tie around the creature's mouth, so it couldn't cry out and draw attention if it woke.

Once that was done, Aron slumped, the adrenaline of the moment draining out of him and leaving him tired again. His heart pounded, but looking back at the battle, he was proud of himself. He'd used the training almost instinctively, and the goblin had been no match for him. If there had been more than one, though… That thought set him on edge again. He drew his sword and tensed, listening for any sign of another attacker. After a few minutes with only the natural sounds of the forest around him, he allowed himself to relax again. It appeared this one had been alone.

Aron stared down at the strange black robes of the creature, the garment that seemed to grant them more freedom than the other goblins, and even the humans, in the camp. He began to form an idea.

Ten

Aron wrinkled his nose as he made his way down the path toward the enemy camp in the fading light. The black robe reeked of goblin, a foul mixture of sweaty feet and boiling cabbage. He longed for some fresh air, but he dared not pull the hood back this close to the encampment. Quite the opposite, in fact; he reached up and pulled it further forward, making sure that his face was as far in the shadow as possible.

He paused in a small copse of trees a few hundred feet away from the entrance to the camp. There were two human guards posted. The light still revealed just a little too much for his liking. The whole plan hinged on his being able to pass himself off as a goblin to get inside and to his friend. The robe would help, but he'd wait for the shadows of early evening as well. He'd seen the goblins in black move as they pleased in and around the camp without being challenged, and he hoped the guards would simply let him pass.

Butterflies made his stomach toss and turn as he waited. What he was about to do was incredibly dangerous, and probably stupid as well. But this was his fault, and he had to find a way to fix it. He felt naked standing there without his squire's sword, but most of the goblins didn't carry visible weapons, and even under the cloak, there had been no way to truly hide it. It wasn't like it would be much help among hundreds of enemies, but he would have felt better having it. His knife hung in its scabbard on his belt, the bottom tied to his leg beneath the robe. It wasn't much, but it was better than nothing.

His plan relied heavily on luck, and if one thing went wrong, he would certainly be reunited with his brothers and father, but it would be in chains next to them. He couldn't worry about that, though. There was nothing else he could do.

That wasn't entirely true. He could still walk away. He knew the smart move would be to find help, but Commander Kyle and the other knights were much too far away. If he could free Doubloon somehow, they could end this tonight. The dragon wouldn't fall for another trick like the net. But the few hundred yards that separated him from his friend may as well have been a few hundred miles, considering the challenges that lay between them.

Though it had been less than an hour, it seemed

he'd hesitated there contemplating his next move for days before dusk finally arrived. He watched the perimeter patrol pass for the third time on their route and stayed put for a bit longer to let them get well past his position. It would be another twenty minutes before they passed close again, and by that time, he'd either be captured or in the camp.

Aron's hands shook as he stepped out of the cover of the trees onto the path that would lead him to the entrance of the camp. He tucked them beneath the robes and sucked in a deep breath, attempting to calm his nerves. That was a mistake, as he also took in a huge whiff of foul goblin odor with it. The stench made him queasy, and he thought for a moment he might lose what little he'd eaten that day. He fought down the urge to gag and tried to settle himself. After a few seconds, he began to stride confidently toward the camp, trying his best to look like he belonged there.

He watched the two guards from beneath the hood as he approached, the situation bringing back bad memories of his first attempt to enter Lanfield. The encounter with the guards there had turned ugly and led to a lot of trouble later. He hoped this entrance went a little more smoothly.

He kept as much distance as possible between himself and the guards as he came closer to the camp. He lowered his head slightly, shielding it more with the hood. He looked straight ahead and moved with purpose, like he had somewhere to be. He passed into the camp and started to breathe a sigh of relief, but then he heard the challenge from behind.

"Oi!" one of the guards shouted. "You're getting back late. Where you been?"

Aron ignored the man and kept moving, but the guard wasn't letting it go.

"Oh, you think you're better than us, do you?" the man continued. "Just because you've got those fancy robes? You're still nothing but a rotten goblin underneath them. Turn around and look at me, you little beastie."

Aron stopped, panic rising, and wondered what he was going to do. If he did as the guard commanded, he would be captured. If the man decided to come after him or raise an alarm, he'd also be caught. Instead, he started walking again, hoping that whatever freedom the robes gave the goblins would be enough to get him through. Apparently not.

"I asked you a question. Where you been?"

Aron paused again, knowing he was going to have to do something. Then, he heard the second guard speak.

"Easy, Thomas," the man said quietly. "It's not worth the trouble."

"The hell it's not," Thomas said. "They're lousy, stinking goblins just like the rest of that lot, and they think they can walk around here and do whatever they want to; think they can ignore their betters."

Aron risked a side-eyed glance out of the corner of

the hood and saw the second guard put a hand on the man's shoulder.

"They can do pretty much whatever they want, and that's been proven. I don't know what he sees in them, but they have his protection. You don't want to get on his bad side."

Thomas started to protest again, but the second guard gave him a hard glare, and he deflated. The two walked back to their post, Thomas grumbling and muttering under his breath about "filthy creatures."

Aron finally breathed a little easier and resumed his march toward the center of the camp where his friend was being held.

HE PASSED a few men and goblins milling around as he approached Doubloon, but none of them seemed inclined to impede him. The men either shied away or spat in the dirt in disgust as he passed, and the goblins who didn't wear the black seemed afraid of him. It was easier than he imagined possible to reach his friend.

As he approached, the dragon cracked open an eyelid.

"What do you want now?" Doubloon asked. "I've already given you my answer several times. It will not change."

"It's me," Aron whispered. The dragon hissed in a breath and lowered his voice.

"You should not have come."

"I had to. I caused this mess. You knew it was a trap, and I made you attack anyway."

Doubloon snorted. "As if you could *make* me do anything."

"I'm getting you out of here."

Aron dug his knife out from under the robes, kneeling at the edge of the net, and he began to saw at it. When that didn't work, he hacked and slashed. The blade had no effect on the heavy cord at all.

"That's not going to help." The dragon stated the obvious.

"What's going on?" Aron asked. "I thought it was silly when they tried to capture you with a net, but… what is this?"

"I thought it was silly as well. I laughed when I saw it ahead of me. But the net is imbued with powerful magic. It's unbreakable. It also keeps me from using my own magic."

"That's why I couldn't talk with you mind-to-mind."

"Indeed. Listen to me closely. There is a powerful wizard at work here. I suspect he is the one who has put together the goblin army. He is the true enemy of your people."

"A wizard? But they're make believe…" Aron trailed off.

"Like dragons and magic?" Doubloon asked, raising an eye. The boy gulped and nodded.

"Now, you need to get out of here. Carry a message to your friend Devan. The wizard tries to coerce me to join his army. For now, he negotiates. I'm sure threats will follow soon. Warn the knights about the wizard and get their help in finding my dam."

"You want me to bring your mother?"

"Yes."

Aron remembered one of their conversations in the valley what seemed like ages ago. "Won't she come anyway? I thought you said dragons could sense when their family members were in trouble."

"We can, but I fear the magic will also keep her from sensing my danger. If she comes on her own, all the better. But we cannot depend on that."

"I thought she didn't like people?"

Doubloon chuckled. "That is an understatement, my young friend. Show her the amulet, though, and she will listen. Do it immediately. Do not hesitate. She is just as dangerous as the wizard, if not more so."

The dragon paused and looked thoughtful. "I would not put you in such peril, but I fear that she is our best hope. Take the knights with you to her home, but do not approach her with them. She will attack them on sight. I'm afraid you are going to have to do that part alone."

"But what about Caleb and Eli, my Da, Gareth," Aron protested. "I can't just leave them here."

"You can do nothing to help them," Doubloon said. "They will be fine for now. I will make it clear to the wizard that if they are harmed in any way, he will never have my cooperation. He is determined that I join him, so that should keep them safe for a time. But bring my dam as quickly as possible."

Aron stared longingly across the field at the tent where he knew the people he'd come to rescue were being held. Would this disguise get him in there? Could he figure out a way to free them? Surely his Da and Gareth could find a way to free Doubloon as well.

"I know what you're thinking, youngling. It will not work. The only reason your disguise has gotten you this far is because it is dark and the guards are lazy. If you go among the black robes, it will be obvious to them immediately that you are not one of them, and there are several inside that tent."

Doubloon's tone softened then.

"I'm sorry, Aron. I have failed you, and now I have to ask much more of you."

The boy fought back hot tears, as he had many times over the last week. He turned back to the dragon. "No. I failed you. You knew. You were right. We should have waited. This is my fault, and I have to fix it. Where do I find your mother?"

"Travel east through the mountains. Her lair is in the tallest peak. I know not what the humans call it, but it towers above its neighbors. You will know it. Show her the amulet. Immediately. Tell her that I call for help."

Aron nodded. Doubloon raised his head as much

as he could and looked behind the boy. Aron followed his gaze and saw two of the black-robed goblins approaching across the field.

"You need to go now," the dragon said.

Aron hesitated a moment longer, wanting to give his friend a hug, or as close as possible through the net. He knew he couldn't. From behind him, there were guttural shouts. He looked back, and they had quickened their pace toward him.

"Come close to me," Doubloon said. "I will provide cover. Then, you run."

Aron leaned in toward his friend, and suddenly, Doubloon lunged against the net, shaking his head back and forth. He managed to clip the boy and send him rolling to the side. The two robed goblins began to run toward them, and behind Aron, the dragon issued a loud, challenging roar.

As the boy picked himself up off the ground, a clamor of alarm went up around the camp. This time, he didn't hesitate. As chaos erupted, Aron ran as fast as he could for the cover of the trees.

Eleven

Aron squinted into the gloom, searching for any sort of landmark he recognized, but he finally had to admit to himself that he was completely lost. He'd managed to flee the enemy camp and make his way back to where he'd left his sword and belongings. After that, he ran south into the mountains, but once he made it into the rocky foothills, he'd lost his bearings. With a new moon and no sun to guide him, he'd quickly discovered that he wasn't sure which direction he was heading. He wished again that he'd paid a little more attention to his father's lessons on the stars. That might have helped.

At least there didn't seem to be any pursuit. Doubloon's thrashing and roaring created such a distraction that it seemed the possibility of an intruder had been forgotten. Aron heard the dragon making a ruckus long after he escaped the encampment and made his way back up into the woods. He had thankfully been able to shrug off the stinking robes when he grabbed his sword and pack, but he wasn't sure the smell would ever leave his nostrils. He didn't know how the creatures lived like that. There was just a hint of chill in the night air, but he was reluctant to don the nice cloak Devan had given him. He didn't want the stench clinging to it.

Aron came to a spot where a ledge jutted out, creating a small alcove in the rocks. It looked familiar, and he was almost certain he'd passed it before. Great. He was walking in circles. With a sigh, he accepted that he'd just have to camp for the night and wait for the sun to get his bearings. This looked like as good a place as any. He longed to put more distance between himself and the wizard's army, but at this point, he could just as well be walking back toward them as away.

The wizard. He could hardly believe what Doubloon had told him. Now, apparently, wizards were real, and one of them had an army. He wondered if Devan and the knights knew about that. Even worse, the magician wanted to bring dragons under his control. Aron couldn't imagine the damage the army of goblins that had threatened his village could have done if they also had a dragon with them. Even Lanfield wouldn't stand a chance against that kind of attack. He had faith that his friend wouldn't give in to the wizard, but what if he had some sort of magic that could make Doubloon join him? Aron shivered in the darkness. He had seen the dragon in action. He didn't want to face his friend on the battlefield, and he knew that humans would not be able to stand against him.

He dug a strip of the salted meat out of his backpack and gnawed on it as he leaned against the back of the alcove and thought. He'd need to hunt for food soon. He was burning through the sticks that he'd brought with him, and it would be nice to have something fresh after a couple of days of only existing on the dried, chewy stuff. He had counted on their mission being quick and Doubloon being able to get game for both of them, if need be. But now, he was on his own.

He considered his next move. When the sun dawned and he had a better sense of direction, he'd have a decision to make. After he found the mountain road, of course. He had no idea where it was, but he thought if he continued to move south, he would eventually run across it. It ran the entire length of the mountains, or so he'd been told. He knew he should do what Doubloon had asked. Make for Lanfield, tell Devan everything he knew, and come back with an escort of knights to find Doubloon's Mum. He'd heard the stories of the dangers in the mountains his whole life, but he suspected there were just as many perils between him and Lanfield as there were between him and the other dragon. It could take him weeks to get back to the capital, and then weeks more to reach that tallest peak where they'd find Doubloon's mother. In that time, anything could happen to the friends and family he'd left behind. The dragon could be under the wizard's control. His Da and brothers and Sir Gareth could be lost.

It made more sense for him to go and find the other dragon and convince her to help. With her on his side, he wouldn't need the knights to free his friends and family. Of course, if he never reached Doubloon's mother, everything would be lost. The knights could help with that…if he could get to them, which wasn't a guarantee. After all, he'd almost been the victim of a goblin very near to Lanfield. But he wasn't the scared kid he'd been back then. He'd be wary and ready for something like that. He had his sword, and he knew how to use it. In fact, he'd just defeated a goblin that snuck up on him a few hours ago—apparently some special kind of goblin at that. He knew he could handle that threat.

He was less certain about what else might lurk along the road. Everyone who lived near the mountains had heard of the wild men, more animal than human, and any number of beastly threats, from giant snakes to fierce cats the size of horses. He suspected that some of the stories were made up, or at least exaggerated, but they were real enough that no one from his village or the surrounding areas wanted to risk the road east through the mountains unless they had no choice, and only a few travelers ever came down from that direction.

As the temperatures dropped, Aron unrolled the blanket he'd brought along and pulled it tight around himself. He knew that he needed sleep. Whatever his decision, he needed to be rested and thinking clearly when he made it. Tomorrow would be difficult. He'd need to make his way south along whatever small paths and game trails he could find. It would be tough to travel over the mountains, at least until he found the road. Even then, it might not get much easier. It was rough close to Lanfield, so he had no idea what condition it would be in this far into the mountains. Did it even exist here at all, or would he find himself on the other side of the peaks and no closer to his goal?

Aron huddled under the blanket, trying to calm his mind and find sleep, but too many thoughts danced in his head. What was he going to do? Was he even now being pursued by the wizard and his minions? What dangers might be lurking out in the darkness right this minute, just waiting for him to doze off, so they could attack? He should try to light a fire to ward off predators, but that would also show the army exactly where he was.

He spent a fitful night with his worries, dozing only occasionally, and usually waking with a start, terrified that what had woken him was some noise out in the gloom beyond where he could see. He kept his sword and knife out of their scabbards and close at hand. But as the sky began to lighten toward morning, no goblins or other monsters came to kill or carry him away. As soon as he was able to see, he stood and stretched. His muscles ached from the exertion of the last few days and nights spent on hard stone, but he knew he had many days or weeks of that ahead. It was something he'd just have to get used to.

He ventured out of the alcove and scanned the horizon. After a few moments, he spotted the smoke of many fires rising into the sky and realized that he had not traveled nearly as far from the wizard's camp as he believed. He had a moment of panic but quickly mastered his emotions. Nothing had found him in the night. Now, at least, he'd be able to see them coming.

As the sun rose over the eastern horizon, he finally had his bearings back. He knew which way to go. He still hadn't come to a decision about whether he was heading for Lanfield or Doubloon's mother, but he had to find the mountain road first. He'd figure out the rest when he got there.

Aron made a quick circuit of the area where he'd camped, looking south, up the mountain. He noted quite a few trails headed that way, and some seemed promising. Picking the one that appeared to be the easiest route for the moment, he set off southward and upward, putting the wizard and his goblins as far behind as possible.

He found himself face-to-face with a giant cat.

Twelve

Aron tossed his pack up, then hauled himself over a ledge and rolled over onto his back. He laid there, gasping for breath, every muscle in his body burning. His hands stung where they had been scraped up from climbing. Briars had grabbed him as he'd maneuvered through thick brush, leaving trails of fire crisscrossing his face and arms. The higher he climbed into the mountains, the paths turned more into very narrow animal trails, and the creatures that survived up here were much more agile and nimble than the young squire. They often crossed obstacles not designed for a young man to traverse, like the ledge he'd just climbed.

The good news was that after a day and a half of hard travel, he'd almost reached the peak. Soon, he'd be headed downward again, which should at least be easier. The bad news was that he'd seen no sign of civilization or the road he was searching for. He'd also seen precious little in the way of game, and the few berries that he'd found he didn't recognize. He knew better than to eat them. His stomach grumbled. He pulled his pack over. He was beyond sick of the meat strips—and he was running low—but it was all he had. He needed whatever energy he could get to keep going.

Aron lay there, chewing and huffing, knowing that he had to pull himself to his feet and start looking for some sort of shelter for the night. Dusk was coming fast. He was so exhausted, he probably could have slept for a couple of days right there on the hard rock. He'd just rest for a few more minutes.

A sound brought him immediately to his feet in a defensive position. It was one of the most terrifying noises he'd ever heard—a low growl coming from very nearby.

He found himself face-to-face with a giant cat. The beast boasted a slick coat of dark brown fur that took on a black luster along the ridge of its back. A line of stripes extended down from that strip near the cat's shoulders, coming to sharp points about halfway down its body. They weren't nearly as sharp as the huge fangs that extended below its chin. Green eyes were fixed on him. The thing wasn't quite as big as a horse, but it wasn't far from it. Aron wondered if he would even make a light snack for it.

The beast stalked back and forth on the other end of the ledge, never taking its eyes off its prey. Panic set in. What should he do? Big cats were not something he had to worry about in the village. He was trapped on the ledge with it, so there was no running. That was probably a bad idea anyway. He thought about the small cats in their barn and how they would chase anything moving fast. He supposed he could jump over the ledge, but it was a long way down. The fall would, at the very least, injure him and make him an easy meal.

He looked to the half-eaten strip of salted meat in his hand and quickly tossed it at the feet of the beast. He tried to remember what his Da had told him to do if he met a bear in the woods. "Make yourself big, never turn your back, and never run." Would that work with a cat? He didn't have a better idea.

Aron gripped his sword in his right hand, for all the good it would do him if the thing decided to pounce, and raised both arms high into the air, standing as tall as he could. The cat sniffed at the meat on the ground before it, nudging it around a bit. Then, it gulped the snack down. It returned its attention to Aron.

"Nice kitty," Aron said loudly. "I'm not food. I'm too big for you to eat."

It sounded ridiculous, and he hoped those wouldn't be his last words. He had no idea what else to do. He stretched up on his tiptoes, adding as much height as he could. The beast watched him and resumed its stalking.

"Go away cat!" he shouted. "You had your meal. Go away!"

Aron shifted his eyes slightly to glance as far to the side as possible without turning his head. He knew better than to look away from a predator, even for a second. That was an invitation. The edge was only a few inches behind him. There was nowhere for him to go that way. With a deep breath, he took an unsteady step forward, toward the cat, hoping the creature didn't see it as a challenge.

As Aron moved away from the edge, the predator lowered itself into a semi-crouch. He held his breath. Would it pounce? Could he react fast enough if it did? It took a slow, sinuous step toward him, still low to the ground.

"Bad kitty! Go away!" Aron yelled at the top of his lungs.

The cat tilted its head and stared at him for a moment. He went to his tiptoes again and stretched, hoping for just an extra inch. Anything that might make it think he wasn't worth the fight. Aron didn't believe there would be much of a fight at all.

The beast sat down on its haunches, still studying the boy. After a few moments, the cat made a *chuff*ing sound. Then, it stood, turned slowly, and with a flick of its tail bounded off over the rocks at a near-impossible pace.

Once the creature was out of sight, Aron released the lungful of breath he'd been holding and collapsed on his backside on the rock, trembling and hyperventilating. He'd fought goblins, met dragons, faced down city guards and bullies, but he knew he'd never been closer to meeting his end than just now. He had no idea why the cat decided not to have him as a snack, but he wasn't going to question his luck. Suddenly, he wasn't so tired anymore. He wanted to be as far away from here as he could before dark. He put his sword away, pulled the pack onto his back and pushed on southward.

Thirteen

s Aron suspected, he traveled faster on the downside of the peak, but it had been another day-and-a-half since the encounter with the cat, and there was still no sign of a road. There did seem to be more game trails on this side of the mountain, and he kept a sharp eye out for the predator but hadn't spotted it again. If the cat was here, though, there also had to be game, and he was hungry. He'd seen a goat at a distance earlier, but there had been no way for him to reach it, nor any way for him to carry the meat. It would have been a huge waste, even if he had been able to take it, and his father had taught him more respect for animals than that. He needed to find something smaller, and his growling stomach reminded him he needed to find it soon.

The day wore on without any sign of a rabbit,

squirrel, or other animal that might provide some fresh meat for dinner. He'd seen a few hawks circling in the sky above, which told him there were likely some smaller critters around, but he guessed he was spooking them with his passage. The rough terrain made stealth pretty much impossible. In hindsight, he probably should have tried to make his way around the bottom of the mountain, but it was far too late for that now. He'd thought heading due south would be the fastest way to find the road, but he'd been wrong.

As he settled down for the evening in a small patch of brush, he nursed the final strip of preserved meat, chewing it slowly to make it last as long as possible. It wasn't nearly enough, and his stomach continued to complain. He took a few small sips from his canteen to wash the salty stuff down. It had also been a while since he'd come across a stream to refill his water supply. It was light as well. He'd have no choice but to be a little more careful tomorrow, even if it meant slowing down.

As the temperature fell, he thought about lighting a fire, but that would require gathering wood and getting it going, and he was so tired. He'd been on edge since the meeting with the cat and had slept even less than the nights before. Every shifting shadow or crunch of a twig in the dark put him on high alert, waiting for an attack any moment.

He pulled his cloak tight around him and huddled under the blanket, curling up into a ball, trying to preserve as much warmth as he could. Finally, he fell into a fitful sleep.

WHEN ARON CRACKED HIS EYES, he was surprised to see the sun already in the sky. He'd woken regularly throughout the previous nights, and he supposed the lack of sleep had finally caught up with him. He shuddered a bit thinking about the cat and whatever other predators might have been out there in the dark. But he'd survived, and he did feel a little better. He sat up and stretched sore muscles, trying to work some of the stiffness out. He took a few more sips from his canteen, but his stomach felt hollow, and he was slightly queasy. Food should be the first order of business. When he set off, he moved a bit slower, watching his footsteps as much as he could in hopes of finding game.

The sun neared its zenith when the brush parted, revealing perhaps the most wonderful sight Aron had ever seen. There, stretching east and west in front of him, was the mountain road. It was narrow and heavily rutted here as it wound its way along the mountain range. He stood in the middle of it for a few minutes, exulting in his discovery.

Aron sat down in the middle of the path and forgot, at least momentarily, about his hunger and everything else. Finally, he could do what he came to do. But what would that be? Doubloon told him to go back to Lanfield and get the knights, and he knew that was the smart move. He looked back toward the west, where more familiar surroundings lay somewhere at the end of the road. But how far away were they? He'd already wasted nearly a week just getting over the mountain and to the road.

He turned and looked to the east, toward his ultimate goal. The great golden dragon's mother, the only creature who might be able to help him rescue his family and Doubloon, lay that way. He didn't know how far away she was, either. It could take him another week or a whole month, to reach that tallest peak. Then, he had to find her lair somehow and convince her to speak with him without roasting him on the spot.

All the hunger, weariness, and despair descended on him at once, and he sat, head in hands, trying to fight back the frustration and tears that threatened to overwhelm him. It was too much. He didn't know if he could do this. But he must. His family and friends depended on him.

The sound of horse's hooves pulled him out of his reverie, and he glanced up to see a covered wagon moving eastward along the road. He shook his head. He'd made a grave mistake while he was lost in his thoughts. He considered darting into the brush and waiting for it to pass, but then he saw the man at the reins lift a hand and wave at him. They'd seen him.

With a sigh, he stood and turned toward the approaching wagon and waited, his mind racing with possible outcomes of the encounter. He tried to calm himself and push the wild tales of the mountain folk out of his mind. Surely, they'd been exaggerated. The couple on the seat of the wagon looked friendly enough. The man wore a wide-brimmed straw hat with a black band around it. His long beard was dark with flecks of gray mixed in. The woman also wore a large hat to shade herself from the sun and a pale blue dress. She gave him a warm smile, and there was kindness in her eyes.

"Ho," said the man as he pulled the reins to stop the wagon next to Aron. "What's a lad like you doing out on the road like this? Dangerous place to be, even for someone who knows the hills, and I'm guessing by the looks of things that you don't."

The lie that he'd formulated while the wagon approached came haltingly to his lips, "I'm headed to visit my uncle."

The man's eyes narrowed suspiciously. "What's his name, then?"

"Devan," Aron answered, the knight commander's name being the first one to come to mind.

"Hmm." The man paused to stroke his beard. "Doesn't sound much like any name I've heard in the hills before."

"He's not from the mountains...not originally." Aron stammered as his mind raced to concoct a story.

"He grew up in my village, but he fell in love with a girl and moved up here to live with her family."

The man's gaze softened, and he gave a sly grin to the woman next to him. "That'll do it every time."

He turned back to Aron. "So, whereabouts does this uncle of yours live? Which mountain?"

Aron had no idea if the mountains even had names. In his village, after all, theirs was just "the mountain." In a panic, he blurted out the first thing that came to mind, realizing belatedly how dumb it sounded. "Tall Mountain."

The stranger's eyes narrowed again. "I see. And what's your name, lad?"

"Aron, sir."

"Well, Aron, I'm Ebbner, and this is my wife, Oma. We seem to be headed in the same direction if you'd like a ride."

"Thank you, sir…ma'am…but I'll be fine. I don't want to slow you down."

The woman spoke for the first time, "You don't seem fine." She looked him up and down, taking in the scraped hands, arms, and face, and she let out a little sniff.

"Those could use some looking to. Ebbner and I were just about to stop for lunch, weren't we?" She cut eyes toward her husband, who smiled.

"Ayup. We were at that."

"I'm sure we've got enough to share, and I can help you take care of those cuts."

Aron started to protest, but his stomach growled again, so loudly that Oma heard it. She raised a questioning eyebrow at him.

"Yes, ma'am," he said. "I suppose I could do with a meal, if it's not too much trouble."

She nodded, and the pair climbed down from the wagon and began preparations.

Fourteen

s Ebbner got a fire going, Oma dug in the back of the covered wagon, pulling out a leather satchel. She shuffled around in it for a few moments and held up a small jar. She studied it, a thoughtful look on her face, and then nodded as if satisfied. Next came a brown bottle. She placed both on the back of the wagon and motioned for Aron to have a seat beside them. He hopped up, wincing as he put weight on his raw hands to pull himself up.

"Let's see those hands first," Oma said.

He held them out to her, and she *tsk*ed. It was the first time he'd noticed how bad they looked, completely raw and red, covered in small cuts and scrapes. She pulled the stopper on the bottle and splashed a little of the liquid on a cloth, which she used to carefully clean his palms and fingers. At first, it was refreshingly cool on the cuts, then he hissed in his breath as the pleasant feeling turned to a burning sting on the wounds.

"It'll get 'em cleaned up," his nurse said. "Sting will only last for a bit."

When she was done with his hands, she ran the cloth up his arms and over the many briar and nettle scratches that covered them. The same stinging sensation ran up his arms as she turned her attention to the scrapes on his face, which was the worst yet.

Oma stood back and looked at him. "That should do. You sit there while I get lunch started, and then we'll finish up."

She pulled a pot and a couple of cloth bags out of the wagon and crossed to where her husband had the fire crackling. They spoke quietly for a moment, then he wandered off to attend to some other chores while she placed the pot over the flames and started adding items from the bags.

Aron let his mind wander as Oma whistled a tune he wasn't familiar with. It reminded him of Doubloon's humming attempt to put him to sleep, and he felt guilty to be sitting there doing nothing while the dragon was in danger. Still, he couldn't help but also feel relieved to be somewhere that at least seemed slightly safe among friendly faces.

Once her preparations were done and the meal was cooking, Oma turned her attentions back on Aron. She cracked open the jar, and he got a big whiff of the contents. It smelled pleasant, almost floral. He found his muscles untensing and relaxing just from the aroma of it. Oma dipped a finger in and came out with a dollop of brownish salve. She took his left hand firmly and rubbed a light coating of the stuff over the cuts and blisters. The relief was immediate. The burning and stinging disappeared. Aron raised his hand, staring at it in wonder. Then, he had an unsettling thought. Was he in the presence of a witch? It would have seemed silly just a few days ago, but now…

"Is it magic?" he asked.

Oma laughed loudly, and Aron looked embarrassed. She just smiled at him.

"No, child. I wish I had a bit of magic, but it's just herbs and plants. The stinging will come back, but this will keep it away for a while and help things heal faster. You should be better in a couple of days as long as you don't go climbing any more sharp rocks or running through briar patches."

"Be careful of the witch." Ebbner had returned, and he gave Aron a wink over her shoulder. "She'll put a spell on you; make you do her bidding. Look what's happened to me."

Oma turned and gave her husband a playful swat.

"You get out of here and let me handle this. You've got work to do before we get back on the road."

Aron stared back and forth between them, unsure what to think. He'd seen his own parents tease each other like that on occasion, but it was rare. His Da was usually so serious. Ebbner didn't seem to be serious at all, giving his wife a look of mock fear before heading on his way. The whole scene made him feel quite comfortable with his hosts. A little voice in the back of his head kept reminding him of the stories he'd heard about the mountain folk and telling him to remain cautious. Well, the stories he'd heard had been wrong about a lot of things, and these two didn't look very wild. They'd done nothing so far but try to help him.

Oma finished tending his wounds, and he hadn't realized just how much they'd been bothering him until the pain was gone. He found himself feeling more relaxed than he'd been since his brothers were taken. That thought snapped him out of the comfortable place, reminding him again of what he was doing here. He shouldn't be relaxing. He should be moving, going for help. He needed to thank Ebbner and Oma and then be on his way. Just as he started to stand, though, the woman returned with a steaming bowl, which she placed on the wagon next to him.

"Careful, that's hot. You'll want to stir it around a bit and let it cool."

He opened his mouth to say…something. He couldn't remember quite what. The smell of the food hit him, and his stomach growled. Oh, right, he needed to be leaving. Well, he could do that after he had something to eat. If he was going to get help, he needed to preserve his energy.

He took a spoonful out of the bowl, blowing to cool it. The stew was full of potatoes and carrots and another vegetable that he didn't recognize, and it was delicious. There were also small pieces of meat mixed in. Aron suspected it was dried and salted meat just like he'd been eating, but in this dish, it tasted nothing like the leathery stuff he'd been surviving on. It was tender and had more flavor of beef than salt. The broth was rich and hearty, and even though he felt he should be ashamed of his greed, he asked Oma for a second helping. She smiled and ladled more into his bowl. He took a little extra time to savor this one, and when he was finished, he was so full that he could hold no more, even though he would have loved another serving.

By that time, Oma and Ebbner had put the fire out and packed everything back in the wagon to continue their journey. Aron went around to thank them for their hospitality and tell them he was going to be on his way, but they wouldn't hear of it.

"No point in walking, laddie," Ebbner said. "We're headed the same way. Might as well hop in the wagon and get some rest. You'll still have plenty of walking to do once we get where we're going."

"I don't have any way to pay for the ride or the food," Aron protested. "I really need to be going."

"Nonsense," the big man said. "Once you're feeling a bit better, you can help me with the horse and other chores if you really want to pay us."

He knew he should refuse, but it made sense. The only way they could travel was east, which was the same way he was going, along the same road. Ebbner and Oma knew the territory, and he'd probably get there quicker than he would on his own.

"Thank you," he said finally, bowing his head toward them.

Oma smiled. "It'll be nice to have someone to talk to besides this oaf." She swatted playfully at her husband again. Aron found himself smiling with them.

"Now, climb up in the wagon and get some rest. We've got a few hours to travel before dark."

Aron nodded and pulled himself up under the cover, out of the sun. The wagon creaked as his two hosts climbed aboard, and then Ebbner said some seemingly nonsense words to the horse. They moved forward, bumping through the ruts toward their destination.

Though it seemed like a perfect situation, an uncomfortable feeling fluttered somewhere down in Aron's now-full stomach. He tried to dismiss it, but it wouldn't go away. Well, he had his sword, and he knew how to use it. He'd stay awake, and he'd stay wary, but he was probably just being silly. Ebbner and Oma had been nothing but nice to him, and it would only be a few days until they reached their home. Then, he'd be on his own again.

Though he fought it, as the wagon swayed and bumped along the road, the movement of the ride lulled Aron to sleep.

Fifteen

After a couple of days traveling with Ebbner and Oma, Aron felt much better. The soreness and stiffness were gone out of his limbs, and the healing concoction that Oma brewed up practically worked miracles on his injuries. Already, the scrapes and blisters were healing over. He wondered if she would share the recipe. If the herbs needed to mix the potion were available near his village, the people would line up for it.

She'd given him his own small jar of the brown cream, which he'd tucked away in his backpack. Oma warned him to use it sparingly, morning and evening, until he was completely healed.

Aron enjoyed the couple's company as well. Ebbner often joked and teased the two of them good-naturedly. Oma's kindness endeared her to him. He'd done small tasks to pay them back for the charity they'd offered him, helping Ebbner gather wood or Oma wash the pots and bowls after meals. She was an incredible cook, almost a rival for his mother. Though the road fare was simple, consisting mostly of root vegetables and a couple of types of preserved meat, it was always tasty.

As he hitched the horse—Redbud, he'd discovered, was her name—to the wagon for the day's travel, he thought that if he didn't already have a family, he'd want one like these two. His mood darkened a bit at the thought of his family. That little feeling that kept bugging him returned. He knew that he'd soon have to leave Oma and Ebbner and strike back out on his own to find the dragon.

They'd camped on a rise, one of the higher points along the road so far, and Aron stared off to the east, shading his eyes and squinting into the morning sun. On the horizon, in the distance, he could see one peak that seemed to stand above all the others around it. He'd first noticed it late the previous afternoon. That, he knew, must be his destination, the place he would find Doubloon's dam. It remained so far away. In the hours they'd traveled, it seemed to get no closer. How long would it take him to reach it? He could still be weeks away.

Yes, he'd eventually have to part with his new friends, but for now, they traveled in the same direction, and he took comfort in being around them. He decided he'd continue with them as far as he could.

"Time to load up, laddie." He turned to find

Ebbner climbing into the driver's seat of the wagon. "We've still got a ways to go."

"How much farther until we reach your village?" Aron asked.

The man chuckled. "I wouldn't really call it a village. We've got a homestead, a few animals, what crops we can grow. There are a few others around, but not too close."

Ebbner looked to the sky before speaking again. "Weather looks good, so I'd say we'll make it home day after tomorrow."

"What about the animals? What happens when you're not there?"

"Neighbor's kid stays at the farm to take care of them while we're gone. I pick up some things for his family to trade for his work."

"How long have you been gone?"

"A couple of weeks. That's usually what the trip takes us."

"Trip to where?"

"Here and there," Ebbner answered. "We make a few stops."

Oma pulled herself up beside her husband and looked at Aron with that warm smile.

"We make the journey a couple of times a year," she added, "spring and fall, to trade for the things we can't provide for ourselves. We stop different places and barter what we can. We always manage to come home with what we need."

Aron thought it wasn't so different from how his parents made deals with other people in their village. His Da needed horseshoes, and the blacksmith needed wool for the heavy aprons he wore to protect from sparks off the forge. Everyone got what they required. He was glad they only had to travel across the village and not through the mountains for weeks. Even Lanfield was only a couple of days away.

"Now, hop in," Ebbner said. "We're losing daylight."

Aron walked around to the back and jumped in the bed of the wagon. He sat there with his legs dangling off the end, as he had for much of the trip. It sure beat walking. He heard Ebbner give the command to the horse, and they were bouncing down the track once again. It had only been a couple of days, but the boy found the movements of the wagon somehow soothing, almost hypnotizing. Despite his initial misgivings, he really was lucky to have crossed paths with Ebbner and Oma.

A hunting trip might be just what he needed to get his troubles off his mind for a bit.

Sixteen

As Aron stacked the wood for the cookfire, he stared off to the east again, finding that tall peak. He fancied that it looked slightly closer than it had this morning, but not as much as he would have liked. Oma approached him and turned her head to look where he was staring.

"That where your uncle lives?" she asked.

He hesitated for a moment, a bit confused by the question, then he remembered the story he'd told them. He couldn't believe that he'd mistrusted them enough to lie. He'd obviously been wrong to be so suspicious. He decided to stick with the story, though. If they learned that he'd been dishonest, they might make him leave, and he really didn't want to part with them before he must—even though that was probably only a day away.

"Yes," he answered simply.

"Have you been there before?"

He shook his head. "This is my first time. Usually, my older brother goes, but he has too much to do around the farm now."

Oma looked at him curiously, and Aron worried that he'd embellished the story a little too much.

"Why does your father send you boys instead of coming himself? What's so important, he'd risk your lives on the mountain road? It's a dangerous place."

"Just messages," Aron muttered, wanting to shift the topic.

"They must be urgent messages."

"Just messages," he said again.

"There are couriers who could deliver them."

"Da doesn't trust them. Afraid they'll take his money and toss the notes. Besides, he can't write."

It was a blatant lie. His father read and wrote better than anyone in the village, but Aron was grasping desperately, trying to keep his story from falling apart. He wasn't doing a very good job.

"I see," Oma said. He could tell by the look in her eyes that she did, in fact, see everything. He glanced away from that gaze, unable to meet it. He wondered what she would do now that she'd caught him in the lie. He waited for the interrogation to continue, but instead, she acted as if nothing had changed.

"I'd better get supper on," she said. "I'll see if I can't put together something for you to take when you leave us tomorrow. You've still got a week's travel ahead after that, if you make good time, to get to...Tall Mountain."

He quickly took his leave, wandering away from the wagon as if he'd spotted something ahead in the road that caught his interest. He wanted to be far from Oma and any questions that might back him further into the corner he'd put himself in. The comfort he'd felt around the couple had slipped. He worried about what they'd do now that he was found out. He wondered if there were authorities out here they might turn him over to. Since they hadn't seen another soul in the days they'd been on the road, that seemed unlikely. What would they do, then?

He wondered if he should try to make a run for it, sprint off into the mountains and disappear. But all his stuff was tucked away in the wagon—his sword, his cloak, his pack. He'd quit carrying it all around the first day when he'd started to become comfortable. He couldn't lose the fine sword and other equipment Devan had given him. What would Gareth do to him if he returned without his issued sword? That soured his mood further. He had no idea if he'd ever see the knight again or become one himself. Everything had changed in such a short time.

Aron started when Ebbner laid a hand on his shoulder.

The man laughed. "You jumped like a deer that just heard a sabrecat growl. Sorry, laddie. What's on your mind?"

"Just thinking about home," Aron said, then quickly changed the subject. "Sabrecat?"

"Nasty critter. Top of the food chain out here. They're huge with big teeth that look like swords. You don't want to cross paths with one of them." Then, he paused, seeing something in the boy's face. "Don't go telling me that you've seen one?"

Aron nodded shyly. "A couple of days before I met you. I was resting when I heard it growling nearby. I thought it was going to eat me. I tried to make myself look big and tossed it a piece of salted meat I was eating. It gulped it down, sniffed around at me, made a funny noise, and left."

Ebbner's eyes widened at the story. "Well, you're a lucky laddie, in more ways than one. Not many folks get to see a sabrecat, and fewer are still around to tell the tale when they do."

The man held up the bow that was in his left hand, showing it to Aron. "I'm fancying some fresh meat for breakfast tomorrow and wondered if you want to go with me to see if we can sneak up on a mountain goat. I could use the help getting it back to camp if we can."

Aron nodded eagerly. A hunting trip might be just what he needed to get his troubles off his mind for a bit. Ebbner nodded toward the brush at the edge of the road, and they headed off in search of their quarry.

THE PAIR RETURNED to camp shortly after dark, tired but happy. They had, in fact, spotted a goat, but they hadn't been able to get close enough for the shot. Aron had stumbled and slid down a rock as they were creeping up on the animal, and it spooked and ran. He feared the man would be angry, but after he helped Aron back to his feet, Ebbner clapped him on the back.

"You did good for a boy not used to moving in the hills. If we'd been on flat land, we would've gotten him."

They smelled Oma's cooking well before they spotted the wagon, and it made Aron's stomach rumble. He'd been well-fed these last few days, but the hunt was the most activity he'd had since he met the couple. He'd worked up an appetite.

Aron gobbled down three servings of the stuff that Oma called hotchpotch. Even though it had been almost the same every night, he hadn't gotten tired of the dish. It was delicious. When he passed the bowl back for his third helping, he looked a bit sheepish, realizing how greedy he must seem. Oma just gave him that smile and ladled out another serving.

After helping with the dishes, he retired to the wagon, stuffed and happy. Ebbner and Oma preferred sleeping under the stars when the weather was nice, but Aron enjoyed having a roof over his head again, so he bunked down under the cover. Oma allowed him to use a roll of cloth that she'd traded for as a cushion for the rough wagon bed.

He nestled in comfortably and was about to doze off when he realized that he'd forgotten to apply the salve to his wounds before going to bed. He started to get up and fetch it, but he was warm and snug. The scrapes and blisters were almost completely healed, and they no longer bothered him at all. Maybe he wouldn't need it anymore. He'd ask Oma what she thought in the morning. For now, he just wanted to sleep. His time with the couple would come to an end tomorrow, so he might as well be comfortable while he could. There would be no hot meals or soft places to sleep once he was on his own again.

Seventeen

〜

Aron slept fitfully. That sense of peace and serenity he'd felt since joining up with Ebbner and Oma seemed to have slipped away. He tossed and turned, dozing briefly, but feeling a growing unease that he couldn't quite explain. He knew Oma, at least, had seen through his story, but nothing had really changed. He had no reason to feel the way he did.

In one of his restless waking moments, he thought about using some of the cream that Oma had given him for his wounds. He didn't think he really needed it anymore, but the scent of it was very calming and might help him sleep a little better. He threw off his warm blanket and crawled toward his pack. As he opened the flap, he heard his hosts talking quietly outside. He knew it was rude to listen, but he couldn't help himself. He needed to know if they were talking

125

about him and what they thought of him now, in light of his conversation with Oma.

"So, do you think this is the one, then?" Ebbner asked.

There was only silence for a few moments, then the man huffed.

"You're being far too picky, as usual. I think the boy would make a fine son."

Who were they talking about? Surely, not Aron. A fine son?

"He's strong-willed," Oma said at last. "He's resistant. He lied to me today, and he persisted even though he knew he was caught. If he doesn't want to join us, he could be a problem."

"Give him more of the calmthorn. Maybe put a little in his food instead of just using the salve."

Aron's eyes widened. He was fully awake now. He couldn't believe what he was hearing. Had Oma been poisoning him with the ointment that healed his wounds? He closed the flap on his pack, no longer interested in the calming effects.

The woman sighed. "I want a son, Ebbner, not a zombie. Soaking into the skin, the calmthorn gives you peace, makes you comfortable. Eating it would take away his will, and we would never be able to let it wear off. He'd know something was wrong."

"Just for a little while. Wouldn't have to be permanent. Only until he realized we were going to give him a good home—better than whatever he's running away from."

There was another long moment of silence.

"What about the sword and cloak?" Oma asked. "They both bear the mark of the King's Knights. If he's a runaway squire, they'll come looking for him."

"Stolen," Ebbner said bluntly. "Look at the way the boy talks and carries himself. He ain't no lordling, and that's about all the knights accept these days. He's so scrawny, I doubt he can even swing the sword, much less know what to do with it. Besides, the knights don't have any real power here in the mountains, and Hezekiah would pay a pretty penny for all that stuff the boy's got."

Anger burned in Aron's chest, and it was all he could do not to jump from the wagon and confront the couple. He'd show Ebbner he knew how to use the sword. The very idea that he'd stolen it and the cloak offended Aron to the core, and the thought of someone trying to sell them…it was more than he could take.

"He seems pretty comfortable with the sword to me," Oma said. "He carries it like it belongs to him."

"Maybe it was his father's or something," Ebbner said. "He still ain't a knight. Boy does have some spine, though. Do you know he told me he faced a sabrecat? I believe him. There was no awe when I described the cat, and there wasn't any trace of a lie in his face when he told the story."

"And you still think he's just a runaway?"

"Aye. I do. Boy's smart enough, and he's scrappy, but he's nothing special."

Aron held his breath, waiting on Oma's response, and it was a few minutes in coming. After a while, she sighed.

"I think you're sentimental because you like the boy."

"Aye. I do."

She sighed again. "I'll sleep on it. If I decide it's right, I'll put a bit of the calmthorn in his porridge in the morning. We can figure out what to do from there."

"Think hard on it," Ebbner said. "He's only the third one in five years, and we're not getting any younger."

The third one? Aron wondered what had happened to the other two. He liked the couple and didn't want to think ill of them, but how much of what he felt was real, and how much of it was the calmthorn, whatever that was? Maybe they had let the other two boys go on their way. *But maybe they hadn't,* whispered a dark voice growing in the back of his mind.

"I will," Oma said with finality. "Now, go to sleep and let me think. I want to make an early start tomorrow."

ARON QUIETLY SLIPPED the straps of his pack over his shoulders and checked to make sure his sword and knife were secure on his belt. He'd waited several tense and torturous hours after the couple had finished their conversation. He wanted to be sure they were soundly asleep before making his escape.

He took a deep breath. The moment reminded him of the night he'd snuck out of his home, headed for Lanfield to become a knight. Only, he'd known his mother and father meant him no harm. He couldn't say the same for Oma and Ebbner. If he'd been caught that night by his parents, the result would likely have been a tongue-lashing and punishment with extra chores. He didn't know what would happen if these two caught him, but he knew that he couldn't stay. At best, he'd end up drugged and kidnapped, basically a prisoner in their home. At worst…well, best not to dwell on that.

Aron felt dumb and guilty for allowing them to trick him. It pained him that he'd even considered staying with them. He knew those thoughts were under the influence of the herb, but that didn't matter. He should have been stronger. He should have been able to resist. Every moment that he'd lollygagged with Oma and Ebbner, enjoying good meals and a comfortable place to sleep, had put everyone in more danger— his Da, his brothers, sir Gareth, his best friend. Terrible things could be happening to them while he was riding the wagon and gorging himself on Oma's hotchpotch.

As he prepared to slip out through the back of the wagon, he looked up on top of the stack of crates and saw Ebbner's bow. He'd grabbed a sack full of the preserved meat and stuffed it in his pack, but it would also be nice to be able to hunt for fresh meat. He had snares, of course, but the bow would give him an advantage. It wasn't very knight-like to take someone else's property, he knew, but it also wasn't very kind to drug someone and kidnap them. Maybe Ebbner deserved to lose something. Though he felt ashamed of himself, he reached up and grabbed the bow and quiver of arrows, then he lowered himself off the back of the wagon, moving as slowly and lightly as possible.

He paused when his feet hit the ground, listening intently. He would have felt more comfortable if Ebbner snored like his father, but sadly, that wasn't the case. He crept quietly around the backside of the wagon, away from where the couple slept, and began to make his way out of the camp. His plan was to follow the road until the sun started to rise, putting as much distance between them as he could. Then, he'd head back out into the brush to try to avoid them.

Redbud whickered as he passed her, and he reached out to nuzzle her nose, hoping to calm her. He wished he'd brought some of the oats from the back of the wagon to give her, but it was too late now. He moved past, and the horse settled, seeming undisturbed. He breathed a sigh of relief, creeping slowly and deliberately away from the wagon. He just wanted to get far enough down the road that he could run without being caught.

He was almost free when he heard what he dreaded, a voice from behind.

"Where do you think you're going, laddie?"

Aron considered bolting, but he knew the taller man would run him down if he did. Instead, he turned to face Ebbner.

"I've got to get to my uncle." He slipped back into his original lie even though he knew the game was up.

"We both know you ain't got an uncle, at least not in these hills," Ebbner said sharply. Then, he softened. "But you could have a family, laddie. Oma and I, we'd treat you well, better than whatever you're running from."

"By giving me calmthorn?" Acid dripped from Aron's voice, and a familiar rage surged up inside of him. He tried to push it down, remembering Gareth's training. He knew things could go badly if he gave in to it.

Ebbner, at least, had the decency to look embarrassed. "You were hurt. You needed the ointment. It healed you, didn't it?"

"And did I need the bit you were going to put into my breakfast?"

The man shook his head. "Heard that, did you?"

Aron nodded. "And I'm not running away from anything. I already have a family. I'm here for them."

"That so? I think you're lying, laddie."

The anger surged, and the truth came rushing out before he had a chance to think about it. "My Da and my brothers are in danger. Sir Gareth, too. I've got to find Doubloon's mother to save them."

"Doubloon? A coin? You have to find the mother of a coin?" Ebbner looked incredulous.

Aron knew he shouldn't say it, but the words came out unbidden.

"He's my dragon."

Ebbner laughed, long and hard. "Laddie, you should have stuck with the story about your uncle. That one was more believable, and I knew it was a lie the second you opened your mouth. A dragon? Really? And you're going to find its mother?"

The man took a step toward him, and Aron drew his sword, holding it in front of him in a defensive stance.

"I don't want to hurt you."

Ebbner snorted. "Fat chance of that. I know you ain't a knight, either. I'm betting you don't even know how to use that thing."

Aron sensed it just in time to twist out of the way as Oma reached from behind with a handful of the calmthorn salve she had intended to smear on his cheek. The distraction was enough to allow Ebbner to close the distance between them. Aron brought the sword up again, darting his eyes back and forth between the two of them, ready to defend against whichever came first. He wasn't sure what to do after that. Neither Devan nor Gareth had trained him to face two attackers. He'd just have to figure it out.

Ebbner pulled a cudgel from behind his back. It was a heavy chunk of dark wood with a large ball at the end.

"Put the sword down, laddie, and let's talk about this. I don't want to have to hurt you."

Aron watched them both warily, trying to form a plan. He leaned slightly forward, as if he intended to place the sword on the ground, then he lunged, lashing out at the man's club with the blade. He knocked it wide but didn't jar it from Ebbner's grip, as he'd hoped. The man growled and reached for Aron with his free hand. The boy twisted away, but his attacker got a handful of cloak, preventing him from escaping. Aron spun back to see the cudgel coming down toward him. He barely got the sword up to deflect it, and the impact jarred his entire body.

Seeing the boy's reaction, Ebbner gave him a wicked smile. "You see, I'm a lot stronger than you. Put it down, and we can pretend this never happened. Keep it up, and…"

The man raised the club threateningly, and when he did, Aron remembered something about fighting that he hadn't learned from Devan or Gareth. In fact, they'd both probably find it quite dishonorable. But they weren't here, and in some situations, you had to do what you had to do. He took his older brother's advice, turning the sword so the pommel faced Ebbner, and then he drove it with all the rage and anger inside him, as hard as he could, into the most delicate part of the man's anatomy.

Ebbner dropped the cudgel and let out a high-pitched whine. Aron didn't wait to see what would happen next. He spun away and was off down the road. On his way past, he snatched up the bow from where it had fallen on the ground, and then he ran like a sabrecat was after him. He didn't slow down for a very long time.

Eighteen

Aron leaned against a rock and gasped for breath. He wasn't sure how long he'd been running, but the sun was well up in the sky now. He also had no idea how far behind him Ebbner and Oma might be, or if they'd even bothered to follow him at all. He could be fleeing from shadows. Clearly, from what he'd heard, he was not the first son they'd tried to "adopt." Would they come after him, or would they just go home and look for another opportunity?

He remained puzzled about the whole experience. They'd been so nice to him. At first, Ebbner seemed to believe he was a runaway and to be sincere about giving him a home. But when he hadn't gotten his way, the club came out. Aron had seen something far different in the man's demeanor then. Oma's, too, for that matter. In those last few minutes, she wasn't the kind and caring person she'd shown him. What would his life have been like if their plan had worked, and he'd ended up addled and living with the two of them as their son? Would it have been a pleasant life, or did they have darker intentions? He honestly didn't know. He realized now just how little they'd shared about themselves and how vague they'd been when he asked questions. As the calmthorn haze lifted, he could see the clues.

Aron looked down at his arms. They'd almost been healed, but now, they were scratched and scraped again from briars and brush tearing at them as he ran. He hoped that he'd stayed at least somewhat parallel to the road, though he doubted he could work up the nerve to go back to it. Ebbner and Oma would be there somewhere. As he rested, he dug the small jar of ointment out of his pack. It could heal the scratches again, but at what cost? The stuff made him complacent and dim, and he couldn't afford that now. He'd wasted too much time already. He needed to find Doubloon's mother as quickly as possible. His lip curled in anger as he looked at the jar, and he cocked his hand back to throw it into the brush. He paused, reconsidering, and stuffed it back into his pack. As much as he despised what it had done to him, it could come in handy at some point…either for healing or its other properties.

He spotted a rock pile up ahead that would give him a good view of the surrounding area. The angle from up there might help him get his bearings, see if he was still close to the road. Maybe he could find out if Ebbner and Oma were chasing him or if they'd moved on. He scrambled up about fifteen feet to the top and squinted back the way he'd come, searching for any sign of movement or perhaps a dust cloud that might show him where the couple was. He saw nothing. He couldn't spot the road through the brush, either, but he knew if he walked south, he'd hit it again eventually. That wasn't the way he was headed.

His head turned back to the east, and he spotted the peak that towered over all the rest. That's where he needed to go, and he could see it well enough from here that he didn't have to expose himself on the road again. It would be a little slower, but maybe safer. Then, he thought about the beast he'd encountered a few days before—a sabrecat, Ebbner had called it. That was a fitting name. He'd have to be on alert traveling through the brush, but that really wasn't any different from being on the road at this point.

Making his decision, he crawled down from the rocks, and having seen no immediate danger, he spent a while resting at the base of the pile. He took a deep drink from his canteen and gnawed on a strip of the preserved meat he'd nicked from Ebbner and Oma's stash. At least he wouldn't starve, even if his meals wouldn't be as appealing as the hotchpotch. He had to wonder if it had really been as tasty as he remembered, though, or if that had just been another effect of the calmthorn.

After a half hour or so, he began to get restless. He shouldn't hang out in one place too long. Aron had neither seen nor heard any sign of pursuit, so he felt comfortable moving at a more leisurely pace. He'd just need to be wary. A slower stroll would also give him a chance to look for something to eat that wasn't tough and salty. He took up the bow in his left hand and nocked an arrow. He could hunt as he traveled. Maybe he'd get lucky.

LATE IN THE AFTERNOON, Aron spotted a welcome sight —distinctive crescent-shaped leaves, almost white at the center, darkening to a bluish green around the edges. The vines encircled a scrubby-looking tree, and his heart leaped. Moonvines they were called, and while they were rare, his family occasionally found one near the base of the mountain back home. The bright blue fruits, hanging in clusters from the vine, were about the sweetest treats you could get in nature. It was always cause for celebration when they discovered one.

He crossed the distance at a run, hoping this vine had ripe fruits. As he got closer, disappointment set in. While it was loaded with berries, most of them were the pale white of unripened fruit, with only a few beginning to show the slightest hint of blue. Those would be sweet as well, he knew, but if you ate them, you would regret it later. The sharp, shooting stomach cramps they caused would give you several miserable hours. He'd never make that mistake again.

He searched the vine with growing frustration, but finally, near the bottom on the backside of the tree, he found what he was looking for—two small clusters of fully ripened fruit. He pulled a pair off the vine, popping them into his mouth. The flavor exploded on his tongue, bringing a huge grin to his face. The berries were super sweet and just a little tart. He took a moment to savor them, then reached out to grab another but decided against it. He pulled his pack off and found a relatively clean shirt. He delicately picked both bunches of ripe fruits, wrapped them in the garment and placed them carefully at the top of the pack where they wouldn't be crushed.

If all he had for dinner tonight was a meat strip, he'd at least have a tasty dessert to look forward to.

He shrugged the pack back onto his shoulders and retrieved the bow. He still hoped he might run across something more filling before dark. Then, he turned east, found the peak that was his goal on the horizon, and started walking again.

As THE SUN began to set, Aron felt good about the progress he'd made for the day. There hadn't been a lot of climbing, and the brush had been relatively light. While that highest peak didn't appear much nearer than it had this morning, he knew he'd moved closer.

Unfortunately, he'd not seen any game during his travels. Hopefully, whatever shelter he could find for the evening would have a few good places to set snares.

A few minutes later, he spotted a large, jagged rock jutting up from the ground with a few scrub bushes at the base. Those would provide a little shelter from the wind, and he could put the stone at his back to guard against anything approaching.

Aron wearily dropped his belongings next to it and tried to stretch out the ache in his muscles. The few days riding the wagon with Ebbner and Oma seemed to have softened him up again. He dug the snares out of a pocket on the pack and struck out from his campsite to search for spots where he might catch a rabbit or other small critter. The area didn't look promising, but he found a few clumps of brush with signs that animals occasionally moved through them.

He wanted nothing more than to just eat and go to sleep, but he was still nervous about whether or not the couple was following him. He needed to at least check. He heaved himself up on top of the rock, where he would have a better view. He sat atop the outcropping until darkness fell completely, scanning all around for any signs of a campfire that might give his pursuers away. Again, he saw nothing. He knew that didn't mean they weren't out there somewhere, but it made him feel better.

Carefully, he crawled back down, feeling his way slowly in the darkness. When he was on the ground, he laid his bedroll out for the night. As much as he wanted to light a small fire, he didn't think it was a good idea, and it wasn't like he had anything to cook over it anyway. Instead, he grabbed a meat strip and began the gnawing that had become a ritual at this point. Once this journey was over, if he ever saw more of the stuff, it would be too soon.

After that, he pulled out the day's prize—the two clusters of moonvine fruits—and laid them out on top of his pack. He picked the fruits off the smaller stem greedily at first, but after a few, he slowed down to savor them a little more. The plump berries burst with the slightest bit of pressure from his teeth, releasing their sweet juices, and Aron sighed, remembering the last time his family had found a few of the vines. His mother made a cobbler from them, and despite her admonishments, he'd eaten the first piece before it had properly cooled and burned his tongue.

The memory turned from warmth to sadness in a heartbeat. He wondered how his Mum was doing back home. She had been hit by two tragedies quickly—the loss of his brothers and the loss of his Da. Now, he'd been gone for weeks as well. He'd seen her state when he left and didn't want to imagine what it might be now. His eyes watered at the thought he might have caused her more pain. He knew he'd done the right thing by going, and if he'd only listened to Doubloon, they might be back home safe now. All of this was his fault.

As he cried, his mind started to drift into a fit of hopelessness. He'd never reach the mountain on his own. And if he did, how would he convince Doubloon's dam to help a human? In her own son's words, she despised them. It seemed too daunting a task. He may as well just give up right here.

An early lesson from Sir Gareth sprang to mind. He'd complained to his master about a visiting knight's squire who shirked his duties. The other boy had been charged with taking care of his master's horse after they arrived. He brought it into the stable where Aron was caring for Gareth's mount, and instead of grooming and feeding the animal properly, the noble boy had simply sneered at him and walked out.

Despite not being his responsibility, Aron had also cared for the other horse because he couldn't stand to see the animal left to fend for itself. The next morning, the visiting knight had inspected the mount and praised the lazy squire for his efforts while the noble boy stood there with a smirk, daring Aron to say anything. As soon as they left, he headed to Sir Gareth to complain.

"I should have said something," he told his master. "I should have told the knight that I took care of the horse."

Gareth gave him an appraising look before he spoke. "Perhaps. But Sir Rowan will learn the truth of his squire soon enough, and speaking up may have earned you the enmity of both. I know Commander Kyle hates politics, but unfortunately, you will be forced to consider them. I fear you have chosen a difficult road already, and enemies will make it that much more difficult."

"It's not fair, though."

"Life rarely is. All you can do is master yourself. Control what you can control. Do what you know to be right. The road will be hard—I won't lie to you—but you can walk it."

Gareth's words were truer now than ever. The road ahead was bleak, but he was doing the right thing—the only thing. In the morning, he would control what he could control. He would get up and strike out east toward the mountain again.

That decided, he reached for the other cluster of berries he'd laid out, but he paused and thought better of it. Those might be the last little bit of pleasure he'd have on this journey, best make them last.

With a last longing glance, he settled in to try and get some rest.

Nineteen

Something skittered in the darkness. The sound had been slight, but it was enough to pull Aron out of his sleep. He shifted his right hand just a hair to the hilt of the sword that lay beside him but otherwise tried to show no sign that he'd heard. He cracked his eyelids to peer around but could see nothing in the darkness.

Though his heart raced, he did his best to keep his breathing slow and smooth, mimicking sleep. He didn't want to let whoever was here know that he was aware. Perhaps those meditation exercises were good for something after all. He listened intently.

Another scraping sound, very close this time. He shifted his head slightly to his right to get a better look at where the sound had come from. In the moonlight, he caught a movement. The figure in the hood appeared to be about his height and thin—not Ebbner or Oma, then. It reached slowly toward Aron's pack. He was being robbed.

In a smooth motion, he rolled over and up to his knees, bringing the sword to bear on the intruder.

"Stop, thief!" he shouted.

A squeal sounded in the darkness, and the intruder stood. It wasn't a thief at all; it was a goblin. He was lucky the creature hadn't killed him in his sleep. Aron came to his feet, keeping the blade leveled at the monster. The goblin stared at him with strange yellow eyes. It puffed itself up as large as it could and released a shrieking battle cry that chilled the boy.

The monster took a step toward him, and Aron took a reflexive step back. The thing smiled, an unnerving expression because it revealed a row of sharp, jagged teeth that could rip flesh. Then, it reached down toward the pack. No, not the pack. It was reaching for the moonvine fruits on top of it. He knew it was a silly thing to be angry about in the situation, but something in the boy snapped. Those little blue berries were the last bit of happiness in his life at the moment, and the goblin was trying to take them away.

With a roar of his own, Aron raised his sword and charged, a rising fury driving him forward. The creature's eyes widened, and it retreated, backpedaling toward the rock. Aron moved in fast, planning the blow that would separate the monster's head from its body. Instead of attacking or defending, the goblin curled up against the stone, cowering and covering its head, a mound of quivering brown and olive muscle.

"No hurt! No hurt!" it yelled.

Aron paused, sword still raised, and stared at the goblin in surprise and amazement.

"You can talk?"

The monster turned to look at him, yellow eyes that had been menacing a few moments ago now pleaded with him; the pointed ears shook and shivered in fear.

"No hurt," it whined. "Please, no hurt."

Aron knew he should finish the goblin. The monsters had attacked his village, kidnapped his brothers, captured his Da and Sir Gareth. They were evil creatures that needed to be destroyed. But as he looked down at the pitiful, miserable thing hunched in front of him, he almost felt sorry for it.

"No hurt..." It was a whisper this time as the goblin curled its body tighter against the rock and turned its face away. It trembled.

The boy lowered his sword. "I won't hurt you...for now. But if you make one wrong move, I will run you through. Do you understand?"

The goblin hesitantly turned its head back toward him and nodded.

"You can speak?"

"Yes."

"Do all goblins speak?"

"Not goblin," it said, a bit of defiance coming into

its eyes, making Aron shift the sword slightly. Its face twisted as it said the word again, "Goblin human word. I koz'thar."

"Kusthar," Aron said, sounding out the strange word. "Do all kusthar speak then?"

"Koz'thar," the goblin corrected, pronouncing the word in a voice that sounded like he had phlegm in his throat. "Yes, all koz'thar speak."

That's when Aron realized what it was wearing— the same black robes as the wizard's goblins. These were worn and tattered, but they were undeniably the same. He reached his sword toward them, and the monster flinched away from it. He lifted the edge of the cloak with the tip of the blade.

"What do these robes mean? I've seen them before."

"Special. Master trusts. Trusts more than humans. Humans only there for gold. Koz'thar loyal."

"But not all gobl…uh, koz'thar, wear them."

"All koz'thar wear. Koz'thun not wear. Koz'thun not bright. Koz'thar special. Chosen. Speak human. Have magic. Smarter."

Aron's eyes widened at that news.

"You can use magic?"

The goblin sagged, some of the pride in defending his race draining away. His ears drooped, and he stared at the ground.

"No. Grottma's grottma was koz'thun. No magic." He said it in a small voice, shaking his head sadly at the proclamation. Then, he raised his eyes and met Aron's defiantly. "Still smart."

"Grottma?"

The goblin looked thoughtful for a moment. "Mother. Humans call mother."

"Why were you trying to steal my pack?"

"Pack?" The goblin scanned the area, and when his eyes found the backpack, Aron saw recognition in them. Then, it shook its head. "Not want pack. Hungry. Get blues."

"The moonvine berries? That's what you wanted?"

The creature nodded. "Hungry," it repeated.

He looked the goblin over again and realized that it did appear quite skinny compared to the ones he'd seen in the wizard's camp. He sighed. He couldn't believe he was about to do this.

"You can't have my berries, but I may have something for you."

The goblin looked hopeful, nodding quickly at the proclamation. "Anything. Hungry."

Aron backed slowly toward his pack, keeping his blade between himself and the creature. He never took his eyes off it. He knelt and tucked the berries inside. He wasn't about to give that treat up. Instead, he removed a strip of the dried meat and tossed it to the goblin. It caught the strip and tore a big chunk off the end, chewing greedily. Then, its face screwed up, and it looked like it wanted to spit the meat out. It forced itself to swallow instead.

"Ruined," it said. "Burned. Sharp on tongue."

Aron pondered that a second. He didn't quite understand, then he realized it must be the salt.

"That's what keeps it from spoiling. Fresh meat is much better, but you get used to it."

The goblin gave him a skeptical look but took another bite. It watched Aron as warily as the boy watched it.

"Listen…uh…what's your name?"

"Name?"

"I'm Aron. What can I call you? I can't just call you gobl…koz'thar."

"Oh," the creature actually smiled, pointing to its chest, "Skrunt. Called Skrunt."

"OK, uh, Skrunt. Tell me about this master of yours."

"Master great wizard. Koz'thar serve. Even above humans. Koz'thar loyal. Carry orders for humans and koz'thun. Help master. When done, he give us home. Place we don't have to be scared. We even let koz'thun live there." When he said the last bit, Skrunt had such a magnanimous look on his face that Aron couldn't help but smile.

"Scared? What are gob…koz'thar scared of?"

"Lots," Skrunt said. "Danger all around. Bears. Wolves. Cats. Humans."

"Humans?"

"Humans worst." A terrified look came over the

goblin's face when he realized what he'd said. "Not you," he blurted. "You share food."

Aron smiled again. "It's OK." He wondered as he looked at the pitiful creature sitting in front of him if other goblins were like this. Had humans gotten them wrong somehow? Like dragons? No, he remembered the one that attacked him in the mountains. That creature had been nothing like the one he was speaking with now.

"So, the koz'thar get a home; what does this master get?"

Skrunt sank even further at the question. He looked as if he wanted to sink into the stone behind him. Then, the monster began to cry.

"Not me," he wailed. "Skrunt coward. Ran away. Can't go back. Master punish. Cause pain. Lots of pain."

The goblin shuddered and wailed so terribly that Aron actually wanted to comfort him, though he had no idea how.

"What happened?"

"We attack humans." Skrunt cut an eye toward Aron, but the boy only nodded for him to go on. "Monster come. Gold monster. Fire everywhere. Gold and fire. No want die. Run."

Anger flashed in Aron's eyes as he stood, raising his sword. This creature was part of the army that had attacked his village two years ago. It had to be. He took a few steps toward the goblin, snarling in rage. Just a few minutes ago, he believed this one might not be as bad as its cousins, but now, he realized he'd been wrong. This monster would have killed his family given the chance. Ones like it took his brothers from their home. He raised the sword.

The sheer terror in the goblin's eyes stayed it for a moment.

"No hurt!" Skrunt wailed pitifully. "No want die."

Aron took a deep breath and stopped himself, trying to find the calm that Gareth had always tried to teach him.

"Go," he snarled. "Get out of my sight. Now."

As he lowered the sword, Skrunt turned and scampered off into the darkness. Aron watched him go as far as he could see, then he slumped against the wall of the rock outcropping and slid down to a seated position. He wasn't sure what to think about the encounter with the talking goblin. A flood of emotions washed through him—rage, pity, sorrow. He didn't know what to make of any of it.

It struck him that he hadn't gotten the answer to his question. What did the wizard get out of their deal? What was he after?

Aron had a lot to think about. It was going to be a long night.

"Come, Quick, Get away."

Twenty

The mountain road wound back to meet him late in the afternoon of the next day, and he welcomed it. He'd traveled through rough terrain for hours, and he was exhausted. He didn't sleep well the night before, for fear the goblin would return. It seemed terrified of him, but Aron knew better than to trust the little monster. He'd eventually drifted off in the early morning hours but slept lightly. Every little noise pulled him back to wakefulness.

Aron still hesitated to commit to the road. It felt more open and dangerous, especially in light of his previous experience. Surely, he had to be past the place where Ebbner and Oma lived by now. They'd said they were less than a day from home, and he'd been traveling for two since he ran away from them. If they were following, he should have seen some sort of sign. He'd stopped to check every time he'd come across a high point where he could get a better look. He'd seen no movement, no dust cloud from their wagon, no indication that they were still out there. He hoped they'd just gone home and forgotten about him.

He glanced to the east again, toward his goal, the peak that towered above the rest. He'd make much better time on the road, where he didn't have to bust through brush, crawl over rocks, or climb ledges. It would also be much easier on his body, which had started complaining again as soon as the effects of the calmthorn ointment had fully worn away. He'd been caught in thorns a couple of times and had been sorely tempted to rub just a tiny bit on the stinging wounds, but he couldn't afford to do that, especially not with a goblin out there somewhere.

After a brief debate, he decided to risk it. Time was of the essence, and the road would get him to his goal quicker. He would just have to remain wary and not let any more travelers surprise him. He'd need to keep his ears open, so he could hide if he heard anything coming.

The road wound steadily downward for the rest of the afternoon, and Aron made good time. He'd likely sleep in the valley tonight and hopefully be rested for tomorrow's journey, which would turn back up through the next mountain in the chain.

That plan changed, though, when he spotted a wisp of smoke rising from the valley, a thin stream, as if from a chimney. He was tempted to get closer and investigate. Perhaps the people who lived there were friendly and would offer him a meal and a bed. It would be nice to spend a night indoors, but the last time he'd gotten a good meal and a bed, he'd also gotten drugged and nearly abducted. They had appeared to be good people, too. It wasn't worth the risk.

Aron cut the day's walk short, even though there was another hour or so of light left. He'd camp on this side of the valley, rise before dawn, and sneak past the houses down there before anyone was awake. He didn't want to be seen again.

He didn't move too far from the road to set up camp. He found a place sheltered by brush a few hundred feet off the path to settle in for the evening. With no fire, no one passing should be able to see him there, especially in the dark. He'd feel much better once he got past the houses and might be willing to risk a fire the next night. At least he'd been able to refill his water. He'd stumbled across a tiny trickle of a spring earlier. It didn't smell great and tasted heavily of minerals, but it helped wash down his salty supper. He pulled the moonvine berries out and picked a couple off the cluster. Those couple of bites of sweetness were the only enjoyable part of his day, and he intended to make them last as long as he could.

Finally, he settled in to rest and was asleep in a matter of minutes.

ARON LAY in the grassy meadow, watching the sheep mill around and feed. He couldn't believe he'd ever thought this life was boring and miserable. It was the most comfortable and relaxing place in the world. The sounds of the animals, the feel of the soft grass beneath him, the gentle breeze blowing past him. No goblins, no dragons, no wizards. It was practically heaven. He knew he shouldn't, but he was so comfortable, he'd just close his eyes for a minute and take a quick nap. It couldn't hurt anything.

Something shook him, and Aron woke in a panic. His Da had caught him napping. He'd be in big trouble again, and he didn't want to have to deal with King Alfred and the pigs. His mind scrambled for some sort of excuse.

But he quickly realized he wasn't in the meadow, and it wasn't his father who had interrupted his nap.

"Wake up. Must wake up."

Skrunt stood over him, shaking him frantically and begging for him to get up. That wasn't a problem. On seeing the goblin, Aron jumped to his feet and fumbled with his sword, drawing it awkwardly. The monster didn't hunker down and cower from it this time. Its yellow eyes were wide, its features panicked.

"Must come. Quick. Danger."

"I'm not going anywhere with you," Aron said.

"You attacked my village. You would have killed my family."

"Killed no one," Skrunt said. "No time. Must come. Now."

"Why do you think I'd trust you? Maybe you just want to lead me to more of your kind."

"People coming," the creature pleaded. "Said Aron's name. Heard them."

That got the boy's attention. "Where?"

"Behind. Maybe hour. Dog with them."

Aron jolted into action, gathering his things and throwing the pack over his shoulder. He started off through the brush to the east, but the goblin grabbed his arm and pulled him toward the road.

"This way."

"No. I can't go back to the road. They'll find me easily there. I need to lose them."

"Trust Skrunt. Know how to get rid of dog. Been chased before."

The boy stared at the creature for a moment. How could he trust a monster that had been part of the attack on his village? But Skrunt was also warning him when he had no reason to do so. Unless this was a trick to lead him away to where other goblins were waiting. He decided that was more likely. He pulled away from the monster, turning again to the brush. Skrunt grabbed him more violently this time.

"They catch that way."

"I don't trust you. How do I know that there are

even people or dogs? You could be lying. Why would you help me?"

"Like you. Aron mean, but kind."

He stared at the goblin again, shaking his head. This was the craziest thing ever, but he believed him. Then, he heard a chilling sound that confirmed the creature's story. Somewhere in the distance, a hound yipped, as if on the trail of something. Skrunt jerked his arm, pulling him harder back toward the road.

"Come. Quick. Get away."

Aron had no idea what the goblin thought he could do to beat a dog's nose, but whatever it was, he realized he didn't have a better plan.

"Do you really know how to get rid of them?"

Skrunt nodded emphatically. "Done before. But have to go. Now."

He couldn't believe he was doing this. The goblin took off toward the road, and Aron followed, running as fast as he could to keep up.

Twenty-One

The very first hint of light touched the edge of the sky as they reached the valley floor. Now, the hound sounded regularly behind them, getting closer each time. While they definitely moved more quickly on the road than they would have over rough terrain, the people with the dog had, too. Their pursuers were steadily gaining.

Aron wondered, not for the first time, if he'd done the right thing in trusting Skrunt, but he really had no choice now. He hoped the goblin really did know what he was doing. If not, they were finished. The speed of the creature amazed him. Aron struggled to keep up, and Skrunt had to stop and wait on him several times as they descended. Now was such a time.

"This way. Quick," the goblin said as Aron caught up. Then, he took off again.

The dog yipped, and it sounded like it was right on

top of them. That put a little added spring in Aron's step as he followed.

He hesitated as a house loomed ahead. He could see the lamplight through a couple of windows, as the residents were up and preparing to start their day. Skrunt didn't slow at all, running right past the home. Aron hurried to follow. The goblin ducked behind the building, and the boy skidded around the corner behind him. They ran across a small yard with a couple of sheds, and Aron spotted another obstacle ahead—a three-rail fence like the pen they kept their sheep in at night. He turned to skirt it, but Skrunt hopped right over. Aron changed direction again, following the goblin.

The fence turned out to be exactly what he thought, though it was much larger than the sheep pen. A couple dozen head of cattle milled around lazily inside. Skrunt slowed down now, and just as Aron caught up to him, the goblin dove into a huge cow patty, rolling around in it and getting the stinking stuff all over himself. The boy twisted his face in disgust, wondering what the creature thought it was doing. Skrunt motioned for him to do the same.

Aron hesitated, and the goblin came toward him, reaching out with a handful of the filth to spread on him. The boy skittered away.

"Hide smell!" Skrunt explained.

Aron crinkled up his face and motioned for the goblin to back away. He understood, but he didn't like it. He'd dealt with plenty of nasty things back on the farm. Heck, he'd even landed face first in the muck of the pigsty a few times. You couldn't be squeamish when you cared for animals. But he'd never done anything like this on purpose. Another howl came from behind them, this one urgent. The hound knew they were close. Holding his breath, Aron picked the nearest cow pat and stomped around in it, getting the mess all over his boots. Then, he fell to his knees, rubbing his legs all around in the foul goop. Though Skrunt kept motioning for him to spread it all over, that was as far as he intended to go. He stood up.

"Let's go."

The goblin gave him a disapproving look but then took off. Instead of running away, Skrunt started making crazy circles around the pasture. He weaved in and out of the cows, seemingly at random, zigging and zagging around, making circles, and turning back where he'd already been. With a shrug, Aron followed his lead.

The boy became nervous as some of the cows bellowed and rustled when he and the goblin ran close among them. While his family hadn't had enough money to own cattle, he'd heard stories about how dangerous they could be when they decided they didn't like something. He didn't want to find out if those were true.

After a few minutes of their crazy dance with the cows, Skrunt stopped on the other side of the pasture.

He pointed across the valley, opposite the way they'd come.

"That way. Run."

Aron took off immediately, ready to get away from the cattle and put more distance between himself and the dog. He was halfway across the open area before he realized the goblin wasn't with him. He slowed and looked back to see Skrunt making another pass through the pasture. On his way out, he whacked several of the cows on the rear with an open hand. The ones that had been struck jumped or ran, which caused the rest of them to become nervous. In short order, they were all making noise, stomping, and moving around the large pen in confusion.

Skrunt sprinted across the field toward him, shouting, "Go. Go."

He turned and ran for all he was worth. Aron reached a tree line on the other side of the field just as the goblin caught up with him. Skrunt grabbed his arm and pulled him to the side, where a ditch ran behind some bushes. The creature shoved the boy into it and then jumped in himself. The water wasn't deep, but Aron's boots sank into the mud as they crouched in the gully. The sky was becoming lighter quickly, and they could see across the field back to the house.

"We should keep going." The dog was getting closer every second.

"No run." Skrunt said. "We move, they see."

"They're going to catch us. We can't just sit here. We need to go."

Skrunt smiled and pointed back toward the cows. "Watch."

A few moments later, Aron spotted their pursuers running around the side of the house just like they had. The dog kept its nose to the ground, only raising its head to bay a few times. Though the light was still low, he was almost sure the man running alongside was Ebbner. He'd never seen the other man, holding the dog's leash, but he was shouting that they were close now.

Their fast progress halted when they hit the cow pen. The hound veered away, following the path Aron had originally taken, then it paused at the fence and turned to look at its handler. The man made a motion, and the dog hopped through the slats and waited. The handler passed the leash through the rails and climbed over, followed by Ebbner. He gave a command, and the dog was immediately back on the trail, until it hit the mass of cows.

The animals remained nervous and skittish from Skrunt's whacks on their behinds, and the presence of the men and the dog heightened that stress. They shifted and mooed loudly as the dog ran to and fro among them. It had quit baying now, and Aron watched in amazement as it worked its way around the pasture, seeming confused. It stopped every now and then, looking back at its master, who would issue a command. Then, it would put its nose to the ground and search more, but it didn't seem to know where to go, making circles among the cows.

Ebbner passed the man a piece of cloth, and the handler held it to the dog's nose for a second and issued another command. The result was the same, and all the while, the cattle were getting louder and more disturbed.

"Too much smell," Skrunt said, looking at Aron almost gleefully. "Told you."

The boy offered a little nod of respect, conceding the point.

The farmer came charging out of his house to see what all the ruckus in his pasture was about. When he spotted Ebbner and the other man among his cattle with a dog, he began to shout at them, asking what they thought they were doing and telling them to get off his property. Ebbner yelled back at him, arguing, but the farmer was having none of it. He picked up a pitchfork and started toward them, and the two men with the hound decided it wasn't a fight they wanted to pick. With a few more words back and forth, they left the pasture and returned to the road.

They worked the dog up and down the road and through the field as much as they could without raising the ire of the farmer and another man, whom Aron assumed was his grown son, who had come out and posted himself next to the cows, watching Ebbner and his friend like a hawk.

The sun had risen higher, and the boy had begun to get very uncomfortable crouching in the ditch and smelling the cow dung on himself and Skrunt. Finally, their pursuers seemed to give up, one of them at least. The man with the dog turned back up the road the way they'd come. Ebbner argued with him.

"The boy stole from us, Jasper," he yelled. "He's a runaway squire, or he stole from the knights. Either way, they'll pay a handsome reward for him. We're close."

The dog handler responded with a harsh word that Aron couldn't quite make out before raising his voice to shout back.

"You're just mad one of 'em finally managed to get the best of you, Ebbner. I'm not wasting any more time looking for another boy that you're just going to use for work until that wife of yours decides he's not the right one, and you send him packing to that orphanage in Lowridge like the others." The man spat in the dirt and shook his head sadly. "Kid's probably better off running through the mountains than in that miserable place anyway."

His piece said, the man with the dog turned again and trudged away, leaving Ebbner looking stunned and lost. Aron's would-be "father" stared up the road out of the valley and took a few steps as if he were going to continue the search. Then, he slumped, looking defeated, and turned to follow the other man.

Aron and Skrunt remained in the ditch, watching

the two retreat until they were well out of sight. The farmer and his son had gone back to their duties by then, taking care of chores that were very familiar to the boy. Slowly, the two fugitives stood and, creeping carefully through the trees, made their way back to the road heading east.

<h1 style="text-align:center">Twenty-Two</h1>

The afternoon's journey stunk miserably, though Skrunt didn't seem terribly bothered by it. The goblin was in good spirits after being right about the dog and saving his new friend. Aron didn't know if he was comfortable with that term, but he had to admit that he would likely be in the hands of Ebbner right now if it hadn't been for the creature. He at least owed him an apology for the other night.

"Skrunt."

The goblin stopped his bouncing gait down the road and turned to look back at the boy.

"Listen, about the other night. I'm sorry I was mean to you and chased you away."

Skrunt looked at him curiously, tilting his head, then he shrugged. "Is OK. Aron nicer than most. Fed me first. Most just chase."

Speaking of food, the boy's stomach rumbled and complained. After the morning's excitement, he'd wanted to put as much distance between him and Ebbner as he could, just in case the man convinced the dog handler to try again. They'd been back on the road for a while, and he knew if they brought the hound far enough, it would pick up the trail. Looking at the steadily rising road, Aron guessed there were no more cattle pastures ahead.

As they topped a rise in the path, the terrain dipped briefly, revealing one of the most wonderful scenes Aron had seen. A clear, running stream babbled through the hills and under a small stone bridge up ahead. He picked up the pace, racing to the edge of the water. He took a handful of the crystal liquid and raised it to his lips. It was cold and delicious. He pulled the canteen from his pack and dumped the stained and nasty stuff he'd been sipping for the last few days, filling it with fresh and clean water. He wandered upstream a short way and found a deeper pool there. Better yet, there were dozens of fish swimming just beneath the surface. This was exactly what he needed to raise his spirits.

He returned to Skrunt with a genuine smile on his face for the first time in a long while.

"Look happy. What find?"

"Everything we need," Aron answered. "Clean water and food."

"Food?" The goblin's eyes widened, and the boy nodded.

"But first, we have to get ourselves clean."

Aron led Skrunt back across the road to the waters below the bridge. He didn't want to contaminate the part of the stream he intended to drink and fish in with the foul-smelling mess they were about to wash off. He stripped off his shirt and pants and waded in. He motioned for Skrunt to follow, but the goblin stood on the bank and shook his head.

"No swim."

"It's not deep," Aron assured him, gesturing to the water at his waist in the deepest part of the stream. "And you need to wash the filth off yourself."

"Koz'thar not wash. Not need."

"Yes, you do. You stink like cow dung."

"No bother. Fine."

"It bothers me. If you want to eat fish, you'll clean yourself off."

The goblin gave him a sullen look and let out a great snort, turning away from the water.

"I'm serious," Aron said a bit more forcefully. "If you want to stay and eat with me, I don't want to smell you."

With a sigh, Skrunt waded tentatively into the stream. He made it out just below his knees and stopped. He crossed his arms and stared at Aron. The boy demonstrated washing, splashing water up on himself and rubbing it around to get the dirt and grime off. He dunked his head underneath the water to wash out his hair, and he heard a great splashing. He surfaced to see Skrunt awkwardly running toward him, panic in his eyes. Aron laughed, and the goblin looked offended.

"It's OK. I'm fine. Just washing my hair out."

Aron managed to get the reluctant creature to clean most of the filth off and at least rinse out the tattered black robes he wore. The boy also washed his own clothes and laid them out to dry, putting on a spare set he had in his pack.

"When eat?" Skrunt asked after they'd finished their bath. "You said clean, then eat."

Aron smiled at him. "Soon. I just have to find something I can use."

He searched the bank of the stream until he found a solid, mostly straight limb, almost as long as he was tall. He used his knife to sharpen one end, turning the stick into a spear. The fish were packed close enough in the pool that he should be able to get a couple with this. He motioned for the goblin to follow him.

Skrunt chirped with happiness when Aron pointed out the fish in the stream. His ears quivered with excitement, and the boy had to hold him back as he ran toward the edge of the water. He didn't want the goblin to spook his quarry. Aron crouched low and crept along the bank until he stood almost directly over them. Holding the makeshift spear over one fish, he thrust it down violently. The school scattered, but when he pulled the stick up, a large one wriggled and jerked at the end of it. He tossed it to the bank and dispatched it quickly, then took a moment to study it. Its scales glistened a shiny silver, and it had shimmering, multicolored splotches up and down its side. He had no idea what species it was, but he hoped it was good to eat.

He stalked the school of fish around the pool for a few minutes until he had two more. Then, he picked them up, collected his pack, and told Skrunt to follow. They traveled alongside the stream for a bit, with Aron instructing his companion to pick up sticks here and there as they went. Around a bend in the stream, they found a sheltered spot away from the road, where he thought it wouldn't be seen, and a few minutes later, he had a small fire going.

He gutted and scraped the scales from the fish and began threading them on sticks to place over the flames for cooking. Skrunt watched closely as he put the first two over the fire. As he started to work on the third, the goblin squeaked and jerked it out of his hand, pulling the prize tight to his chest.

"No ruin," Skrunt said, then took a big bite out of it.

Aron wrinkled his nose in disgust, but when he saw the light of happiness in his companion's eyes as he chewed, he couldn't help but smile. He was reminded of Doubloon's aversion to cooked meat.

"Good," the goblin said when he swallowed his bite. Then, he tore off another chunk.

The boy leaned back, watching the fire and savoring the smell of his dinner cooking. A strange feeling came over him. Contentment. Despite the stakes of his journey and the difficult path that lay ahead, in this moment, for at least a little while, he was content.

When the skin of the fish began to blister, he pulled them from the flames. Gingerly, he picked a piece off with his fingers, blowing on it to cool it. His stomach grumbled, telling him to gulp it all down, but he knew better. When he finally took a taste, it was still piping hot, but not enough to burn. The clean white flesh melted in his mouth. He hadn't eaten a lot of fish in his life, but this one was definitely the best he'd ever tasted, even better than the ones in Doubloon's valley. It was a struggle not to wolf the rest of it down and burn himself.

When he finished the first, he reached for the second. Then, he remembered his companion. He pulled a piece off and held it out, offering it to Skrunt. The goblin took it reluctantly and sniffed at it. He popped it into his mouth, and a series of expressions flashed across his face, but the last one was certainly not pleasant. Aron offered him another bite, but the creature shook his head violently and returned to his raw fish. The boy shrugged. More for him.

Once the meal was done, he pulled the last of the

moonvine fruits out of his pack. They were beginning to go soft, but he was determined to make them last. There were six left. He plucked three of them. They were still just as sweet and juicy, and given the relative bounty and safety they had now, these might have been the best of the bunch. He started to tuck the final three away, then he looked over to the goblin who had possibly saved his life. He sighed. Then, he turned and offered the final berries to Skrunt.

The creature looked confused and, at first, didn't move to take them.

"It's OK," Aron said. "I want you to have them."

Skrunt reached out cautiously and took the stem with the now darker blue berries. He hesitated, looking to Aron again for approval as he began to pluck the first one. The boy nodded encouragingly. The goblin placed the fruit delicately into his mouth and bit into it. His eyes widened as he chewed, and then a huge, goofy grin split his face. Aron laughed at the expression. He understood completely. While he hadn't liked the cooked fish at all, Skrunt seemed to have the same sweet tooth. Just like Aron, he savored the last two berries, then laid back with a contented little sigh. Aron watched him for a few moments, until the goblin realized he was looking.

"What?"

"Are the other gobl...koz'thar like you?"

Skrunt pondered that for a few seconds.

"Some," he said, a sad look coming over his face. "Few. Most think Skrunt weak."

"Well, they're wrong," Aron said.

A small look of pride came over the goblin's face, but just for a second. Then, he held up the empty stem that had held the moonvine berries.

"Find more tomorrow."

Aron laughed.

Twenty-Three

The days that followed their flight from the hound passed mostly uneventfully. They had to leave the road a couple of times because of travelers, but luckily, Skrunt had excellent hearing and warned Aron of the danger long before it arrived. All the people they encountered passed right by their hiding spots without a second glance, and to the boy's relief, none of them had been Ebbner.

They were well-fed. Aron had speared and cooked a few more fish for breakfast and lunch on the day they left the stream, and one night, he'd been lucky enough to catch a rabbit in one of his snares. He had to cut it in half because Skrunt wouldn't even entertain the idea of having his portion cooked.

Despite his limited conversational skills and penchant for raw meat, the goblin—no, koz'thar, Aron had to keep reminding himself—proved to be quite likeable and handy to have on the journey. Skrunt could scramble up the rocks much quicker and easier than Aron, and at least most of the time, the boy could translate what his companion was attempting to report. The only thing that really concerned them were people. They'd put miles between them and his would-be adopted family, but Aron was still nervous they would show up.

For his part, Skrunt scouted away from the road regularly, and while he pretended to be looking for threats, Aron suspected the creature was actually searching for another moonvine. So far, he'd been disappointed. He didn't want to dash his companion's hopes, but Aron knew just how rare a find they were, at least around his village. And just because you found one didn't mean that you'd find another there later. His Da's theory was that migrating birds carried the seeds from somewhere else, and, just occasionally, one would take root and grow.

Today was a downhill day, so it had been an easy walk, and the highest peak appeared much closer than it had been. What he'd thought hopeless a relatively short time ago now seemed in reach. Aron had to admit that having a traveling companion had also buoyed his spirits. He'd used the time to begin learning about Skrunt's background and goblin society. The koz'thar were more like his associate, in that they were smarter. They could be taught to communicate with humans, and most had magic of some sort. Skrunt had been a disappointment to his family because he had none. He blamed his grandmother, who was koz'thun. They made up the majority of the species, the fierce and feral goblins he'd met before. The koz'thar looked down on their cousins but still felt the responsibility of kinship. When they got their reward from the wizard, they would open their new home to their rougher relatives.

As for the magician himself, Aron hadn't learned much more. He'd been enjoying his conversations with Skrunt, so he hadn't wanted to push too far. When the subject came up, his companion went quiet. He felt disgrace at fleeing Doubloon's attack and running away from the army, and he also feared the wizard's retribution. Having been there to see the devastation the dragon left in his wake, Aron didn't understand how anyone could be blamed for running away. What he'd seen that day was a side of his friend that he still struggled to reconcile with the warm and welcoming Doubloon he'd grown to love.

His thoughts were interrupted by the koz'thar returning from one of his scouting missions.

"Need camp. Humans ahead."

He pointed down into the valley they were descending, and Aron nodded his understanding. They'd skirted homesteads in every low area they'd passed through.

"More danger," Skrunt added. "Humans talk about monster."

That news concerned Aron more. Houses were no big deal. They could sneak past in the night. People were scattered, and there was no watch set out here. Despite the reputation that the road through the mountains had back home, the dangers had been relatively few so far, and most of them human.

"What kind of monster?"

"Not know. Humans say blocking road."

That was decidedly not good news. He hoped Skrunt would be able to spot whatever it was in his scouting and get them around it before they were in danger. He didn't want to leave the road again. They were making excellent time, but it didn't seem they would have much of a choice.

"Well, we'll figure it out when we get there," Aron said. "First, we've got to get past the houses. Let's find a spot to rest."

An uncomfortable feeling settled on him as they entered.

Twenty-Four

They passed the handful of homesteads in the valley easily in the pre-dawn hours. All was dark and quiet. By the time the sun began to lighten their surroundings, they were climbing again. The great peak loomed large ahead of them, taller and more jagged than the surrounding mountains. If Aron's guess was right, the mountain they were currently winding their way around would be the final obstacle before they reached their destination. It may also prove to be the hardest. He had no idea what kind of monster might be blocking the road ahead or if they would be able to avoid it. He hoped the chatter Skrunt heard from the people in the valley had been exaggerated, like his own village's stories about the dangers of the mountain road.

It was nearing noon when the terrain began to change. Jagged rocks rose up on either side. Aron wasn't sure what could have created such a gash in solid rock, but the road seemed to have been built right through it. An uncomfortable feeling settled on him as they entered. If they continued this way, there would be no getting off the road if they ran into another traveler. By the time they climbed the rock face to either side, whoever was coming would be on top of them. If he were a monster, this was exactly the kind of place where he'd set an ambush—somewhere it would be difficult for anyone to escape.

Aron paused before stepping into the shadow of the corridor. Skrunt continued, unbothered, until he realized his companion wasn't coming. Then, he turned questioningly.

"Not coming?"

"I don't like this at all. It looks like the perfect place for a trap."

"Scout?"

"I think so, but not on the road. Go up top, make sure that monster you heard about isn't blocking the way."

Skrunt nodded and scrambled up the rock face, bouncing along the top. Aron shook his head. As reluctant as he'd been to accept the creature, he wasn't sure how he would get along without his companion at this point. If he'd somehow managed to evade Ebbner, he would have certainly blundered into other problems, whether at one of the houses they'd passed or with whatever monster might be ahead.

Once the koz'thar was out of sight, Aron pulled back from where the walls began to rise and settled himself, hidden, a little off the road. He pulled out a strip of the dried meat that he'd stolen from Ebbner and Oma. They were again running low now that he was feeding two. He should try to hunt while he was waiting on his scout to report back. Once he finished lunch, he strung up Ebbner's bow and stalked the scrub around the road, looking for anything that might provide a meal.

With the sun sinking low, he'd still not managed to spot any sort of game. More concerningly, Skrunt had not returned, either. He was rarely gone from the road for more than an hour or so before coming back to check in. Aron was worried. What if the koz'thar had fallen and hurt himself? The way he bounced along those rocks with abandon, there was always a chance he could have made a mistake and fallen. Or worse. What if whatever was waiting up ahead had caught him sneaking around?

His nervousness grew as full night fell, and the moon began to rise in the sky. Skrunt should be back. Something had happened. Aron knew that he should wait until morning to go looking for his companion, but he couldn't help himself. The koz'thar could be in trouble, and it might be too late by the time the sun came up. He pulled himself up and took the same route up the ridge.

Aron traveled much more slowly and carefully

across the top of the rocks. They were rough with lots of gaps that he either had to jump over or maneuver around. When he had the choice, he would push further away from the road to get past them, but in a few places, he had no option but to make the leap. The landing on the precarious stones was always uneasy, and at least twice, he'd barely caught himself before sliding down. Despite Skrunt's obvious agility, he saw how easily it would be to fall and get hurt, or worse.

He began to peer down at the road every time he came to one of those spots. At the highest point of the ridge, it was about a twenty-foot drop. He dreaded finding the koz'thar lying down there and wondered how he would get to him to help if this worst fear came true. There was no climbing the rocks here, at least not without a rope, which he didn't have. The one he'd brought from home had been used to tie the goblin up at the wizard's camp. The walls of the pass were unnaturally smooth, and Aron wondered again what could have created the narrow canyon. He would have guessed water, but there was no sign of it. Whatever carved this must have been ancient because it had clearly been here before the road, and the builders must have decided it was a convenient route.

Looking at the moon, Aron guessed he only had a couple of hours before dawn. He'd been picking his way carefully along the ledge for most of the night, and he was exhausted. There had been no sign of Skrunt. He wondered if maybe his companion had abandoned him. Maybe he had met up with more of his own kind and decided to leave the human to his own devices. That thought chilled him for a second. If there were goblins wandering around up here in the dark, he could be in serious trouble. After their days on the road, he couldn't imagine Skrunt betraying him, though.

He paused when he saw a faint glow down below on the path ahead. Staying as low as he could, he approached slowly and cautiously. The source proved to be a fire, sheltered behind a pair of huge boulders that had been placed across the road, barring access through the pass. This must be the roadblock that Skrunt heard about. Aron flattened himself as much as he could and crawled forward to peer down onto the scene.

A terrible sound rose up from the road below, and Aron traced it to a figure lying with its back against the boulders. His eyes widened as he saw the scale of the massive monster. It had to be at least ten feet tall. A giant? There were stories about those on the road. Except for the size, its shape looked human. It grunted and shifted its head in its sleep. The noise paused for a moment, but then it continued as before. Aron realized it was snoring. The head turn also gave him a better look at the face. While that also looked mostly human, great tusks jutted from its lower jaw, almost like a goblin, only each of them was nearly as big as Skrunt. A great mane of greasy black hair was tied back, and it wore only a loincloth, which also frightened Aron when he recognized a set of tell-tale stripes decorating it. He'd seen those before. The giant wore the skin of a sabrecat. That most certainly meant it was a fierce fighter.

Aron scanned the camp and spotted two figures lying on the ground near the fire. One appeared to be a human, and it looked like he was either asleep or possibly dead. A second, smaller one struggled mightily against its bonds, and his heart caught in his throat. Down there, on the road, in the lair of the monster, lay Skrunt.

Twenty-Five

Aron continued along the edge of the drop for another hundred yards or so until he finally came to a spot where he thought he might be able to climb down to the road. There was a crack in the wall big enough for him to wedge himself into and try to shinny down. The drop was only about ten or twelve feet here, so if he did fall, perhaps he wouldn't be hurt too badly.

He wouldn't be able to climb down with his pack and other belongings, though, and there would be no way to get back up here—at least not quickly. He considered his options. Kneeling, he dug into the bottom of the backpack and took out the amulet that Doubloon had gifted him. It was the single most important possession he had right now. Without it, he would not be able to convince his friend's mother to help them. More likely, they'd get roasted instantly. He placed it around his neck and tucked it inside his shirt to make sure it was safe. He touched the jar of calmthorn ointment and considered for a second, then he also took it out and put it in his pocket. It was the only breakable thing he had, and he still thought it might come in handy. Then, he tightened his belt, so he could keep his sword and knife on him. Everything else, he could do without if it came to that.

He leaned over the edge and dropped the pack to the road below. He winced at the *whop* it made when it landed and froze, listening to see if anything else might have heard. After a few moments without any sound from the direction of the monster, he relaxed. He then took the bow by the end and lowered it as far as he could before letting it also drop. When it struck the ground on its end, he heard a sickening crack. It bounced back up and then clattered off across the road. He knew the bow was done, but he dropped the quiver over the side as well, just in case, and saw the arrows scatter as they landed. Then, he squeezed himself into the crack and began to work his way down.

The walls inside the crevice were not quite as glassy smooth as the side walls, and he shinnied his way down much more easily than he'd expected, using his back and legs. He ended up in an awkward position at the bottom, which led to an ungraceful face-first fall onto the road to get out, but he made it. Now what?

He located the bow, and as he'd feared, a wide

crack ran up nearly the entire bottom half. It was useless. At least he still had his pack. There was nothing breakable in it. And he had the most important thing around his neck.

With a deep breath and a small prayer, he began to creep back down the road toward the monster and Skrunt. When he got close enough to hear the great giant's snores again, he relaxed just a little. Maybe he could still get out unnoticed. He'd sneak in, cut the koz'thar's bonds quickly, and then they'd run faster than they had from Ebbner's dog. With any luck, they'd be far away by the time the thing woke.

As he inched closer to the roadblock, Aron began to see the bones scattered around on the edges of the road. There were a lot of them. He spotted what looked like deer, and maybe cows. He saw others that most definitely did not look like animals. He tried not to think about that as he came within view of his companion. The monster still snored loudly. Before he could lose his nerve, Aron ducked low and crept along the wall toward Skrunt.

The koz'thar's eyes widened when he saw the boy, and Aron held up a finger over his lips in warning. He crossed the area to Skrunt as quickly as he dared, and in a few moments, he had his companion's hands and feet free. The creature rose to his feet, shaking arms and legs to return the circulation. Aron motioned for him to follow and started back down the road. Then, he heard a muffled sound from nearby and turned to look at the man who was also tied up. He gave the pair a desperate, pleading look.

The monster stirred in its sleep again, and Aron tensed, preparing to bolt, but it soon resumed its snoring. The boy didn't know if he could trust the stranger. Doing that had gotten him in trouble recently. But he remembered the bones littering the road. The easiest, and possibly safest, thing would have been to leave him there and run, but he knew that was not what a knight would do. He couldn't leave the man to that fate. Still, that didn't mean he had to trust him.

He handed his knife to Skrunt, handle first, and motioned for him to cut the man's bonds. Aron drew his sword, holding it threateningly, prepared to defend himself if need be. He knew if it came to that, they'd likely all be dead soon with the giant looming over them.

The stranger's eyes widened in panic as he saw Skrunt approaching him with a knife. Aron shook his head and held out a placating hand, hoping to calm the man. He squeezed his eyes tightly as the creature came close, and the boy understood his fear. A few days ago, if he'd seen a goblin approaching with a knife, he would have felt the same. The koz'thar made quick work of the ropes that bound the man, retreating in a hurry to where Aron stood, sword at the ready. The stranger, obviously expecting an attack, looked surprised to find that he was now free. He stood slowly, shaking to restore feeling, just as Skrunt had.

The boy and the koz'thar began to back down the road slowly and quietly, Aron keeping an eye on the man as he followed, but he made no threatening moves. When they finally got back to where Aron had left his pack, he stopped near it. The stranger kept moving right past them, holding his hands up to show that he wasn't going to hurt them. Once he passed them, he broke into a run. Aron scooped up his things, and he and Skrunt did the same.

The unnatural canyon ran for another quarter of a mile or so, and then, they were back out in the open on the side of the mountain. The man stood there waiting for them. Aron slowed and dropped his hand to the hilt of the sword again, but the man held his own hands up.

"I just wanted to thank you," he said. He eyed Skrunt strangely before adding, "Both of you."

"You're welcome?"

"What's a boy your age doing in the Dragon's Pass?"

"Dragon's Pass?"

The man motioned to the strange canyon they'd just emerged from.

"The legends say a great, ancient dragon burned the mountain itself to create it, and you'll find old-timers in the hills who believe that dragons still live up on Skyclaw Mountain." He hooked his thumb toward the high peak that was their destination. Aron noticed for the first time that it was, indeed, shaped a bit like a giant claw. "That's foolish, of course. Don't know what actually made it, but I know it wasn't dragons."

Aron chuckled nervously. He wasn't so sure.

"Anyway, name's Hobart, and you're welcome in my home any time. Even the goblin."

Skrunt twisted his face up at the word, but Aron shook his head. Now was not the time.

"If anyone comes asking, just don't tell them you've seen us," Aron said.

Hobart studied him for a while with a strange look on his face, but then he nodded.

"Because of you, I'll get to hug my son again tonight. I didn't think that was ever going to happen." The man smiled at him. "Kid, I ain't seen nothing, and if you did come this way, you probably got eaten by the ogre."

So, that's what the thing was. Aron had, of course, heard stories about the monsters, but he'd always pictured them as green-skinned and a bit fatter and clumsier than the muscular giant he'd rescued the man and Skrunt from.

Hobart gave them a little salute, and then he turned north, leaving the road, presumably to go around Dragon's Pass and the ogre. Aron breathed a sigh of relief. He'd managed to save Skrunt and not get himself killed in the process. He also now knew the name of his destination and seemed to have confirmation that there might be a dragon in residence. Things had gone better than they had any right.

He turned back to the koz'thar, who was handing the knife back to him.

"Save me. Thank you."

Aron smiled at him, finally accepting something he'd been fighting for days now.

"That's what friends do," he said.

Twenty-Six

Aron debated leaving the road but decided speed would be more useful than hiding when the ogre awoke to find his breakfast missing. They moved as quickly as they could, not quite running, but keeping a steady pace. They stopped for nothing through most of the day, and by late afternoon, he was almost dead on his feet. Their flight had slowed to a shuffle. He'd not slept the night before, and he doubted that Skrunt had, either. A glance to his companion confirmed that his energy was flagging as well.

"We need to find a place to camp."

"But ogre."

"I think we're far enough away now. If he was coming after us, we'd know. Besides, it doesn't matter if we're too exhausted to run when he catches up with us. We need rest."

Skrunt looked like he was about to argue, but then he nodded.

"Scout first." Aron said, and the koz'thar scrambled off the road toward a higher point as the boy began to look for a suitable spot that would give them some cover to sleep.

About half an hour later, Skrunt came skidding to a stop in front of him, clearly in a state of panic. Before Aron could open his mouth to ask what the problem was, the creature blurted it out.

"Ogre coming! Look angry!"

An image of that monstrous face twisted in rage came unbidden into Aron's thoughts. They were so close to their goal. He guessed they'd reach the base of Skyclaw Mountain early tomorrow, and maybe in another day, they could be on their way to save everyone and go home. Skrunt broke him from his thoughts by grabbing his arm and pulling frantically.

"Must run!"

Aron shook off the frustrated thoughts. All was not lost. They just had to figure out a way to escape the ogre. The two of them took off, the koz'thar in the lead. He'd never seen the creature move as fast as he was now, not even when they'd been fleeing the dog. What he'd seen and been through obviously frightened him, and that scared Aron as well. As the adrenaline of fear surged in him, the weariness faded to the background. He pushed himself hard to keep up with his friend.

That burst of energy wore off as the mountain that was their goal loomed just ahead. Aron's legs burned, and he breathed in heavy gasps. Their pace had steadily slowed for the last half mile or so, and he didn't know how much longer they would be able to hold out. He risked an occasional glance over his shoulder, but he'd seen no sign of pursuit yet. He didn't know how far behind them the ogre had been when Skrunt spotted it, but he knew that, just by the gift of its size, it could move much faster than they could. He was tempted to call a halt and send the koz'thar to scout again, see if it was still behind them, but he also feared the delay. It was inevitable, though. If they didn't rest soon, they'd collapse. Then, they'd be easy prey for the monster.

At the foot of Skyclaw Mountain, Aron found what might be their saving grace—the entrance to a cave. He motioned to Skrunt, and they put on a final burst of speed to reach it. Ducking inside, Aron collapsed against the wall, shaking and gulping in huge breaths. His companion was not in much better shape. If they were lucky, the ogre might pass them by while they hid there. If not, it would at least be a little harder for him to get to them. The roof of the cavern was only about six feet tall, and it was not very wide. He would have to crouch to get in, which might give them an advantage.

Aron peered into the darkness beyond the entrance, remembering the last time he'd taken shelter in a cave. That one held good secrets. He hoped this one might, too. If it went anywhere, they could almost certainly escape the ogre, but he wasn't quite ready to go exploring just yet. First, he wanted to be sure that the monster was actually still pursuing them. They could rest here for a little while and hope that it had given up. If not, he would risk going deeper into the cavern.

He was just about to share that plan with Skrunt when he heard the unmistakable thud of heavy footsteps running up the path they'd just fled. Both of their eyes shifted back to the road in time to see the ogre jogging his way toward them. Aron pulled his friend further into the darkness.

"Maybe he'll pass us," he whispered. Skrunt looked skeptical.

As the monster drew even with the cave, he slowed to a walk, studying his surroundings. He continued along the road past them, and Aron breathed a sigh of relief. It proved to be short-lived, as Skrunt clutched his arm a few moments later. The ogre was back and standing at the spot where they'd left the path. It knelt, examining the ground. Then, it raised its ugly mug and sniffed at the air. It looked straight toward where they hid, stood, and came for them.

"Go!" Aron said, pulling Skrunt deeper into the cave. Though he longed to run, once they were a short distance from the opening, he could barely see his hand in front of his face. It would do no good to escape the ogre and tumble into a hole filled with sharp stalagmites. He moved as fast as he dared, testing his footing with every step and keeping a hand in front to feel the way. Then, disaster struck. He met a solid wall only about twenty-five or thirty feet in. He felt both ways along it, but it was a dead end. Remembering the cave above Doubloon's valley, Aron frantically pushed at random rocks on the wall, hoping one of them would open a secret passage. He had no such luck this time. This was just a natural cave, and they were trapped.

He glanced back toward the entrance, which was mostly blocked by the ogre's body as it tried to squeeze inside to come after them. Aron drew his sword and waited. The cave narrowed even more toward the back, and it would be a tight fit for the monster. Even if he managed to somehow slay the beast, they were still probably trapped. There would be no getting past him to get out. Their only real hope at this point was for the ogre to give up. Even then, it would likely just wait for them outside the cave; they'd have to leave eventually.

The monster reached through the entrance to the cavern, swiping back and forth with its massive arm, but they were well beyond its reach. It would have to try to come in after them. The ogre leaned down, attempting to make itself as small as possible and started to stuff its body inside the entrance. In he came, seemingly folding in on himself. Where the cave narrowed, the beast stopped. It grunted and shifted, then shifted again. The monster began to struggle frantically, and Aron realized that it was stuck. He thought about attacking but then reconsidered. While the ogre was mostly defenseless, there was still the matter of him and his friend escaping.

He watched as the ogre struggled, finally backing itself up enough that it had some room to maneuver. It studied the opening for a minute, turning its head back and forth. Then, it took a slightly different angle, pushing toward them again. Aron sucked in his breath, but once again, the monster got stuck. After a few minutes of struggle, it extricated itself. The beast threw itself at the opening in a fury, its clawed hand reaching as far as it possibly could, but still far away from reaching its quarry.

It lashed out that way for a few moments before finally realizing the futility of the effort. It slowly backed completely out of the cavern, and sat down, staring toward them. The ogre threw its head back and released an ear-splitting roar. The sound reverberated through the small cave, nearly deafening Aron and Skrunt. The boy knew the monster wouldn't give up, and he wondered what would come next. He assumed it would be a waiting game, and it was one the ogre was likely to win.

A great rumble began from somewhere above them. From the top of the mountain, another roar answered the ogre, a louder, more primal sound that seemed to vibrate the very stones around them to their core. The monster at the cave door stood quickly, stumbling backward, and looked up. The blood-chilling shriek sounded again, and Aron recognized it for what it was. He'd heard a similar sound come from Doubloon when the dragon had defeated the goblin army outside his village.

With the second cry, the ogre broke and ran, its footsteps thudding away back down the road. Aron breathed heavily and relaxed, then he turned to find Skrunt huddled on the floor of the cave in sheer terror. He shook violently, eyes wide, as he curled into a ball, perhaps remembering the same moment of Doubloon's attack. Aron reached down and placed a reassuring hand on his friend's shoulder.

"It's all right," he said gently. "She's the reason we're here."

Twenty-Seven

"No."

Skrunt planted his feet, crossed his arms, and glared at Aron. His narrowed eyes resembled his dangerous cousins far more than the companion the boy had come to respect over the last few days.

"Gold. Fire. No."

The koz'thar had refused to budge from the mouth of the cave since they'd heard the dragon's roar high above. Skrunt recognized it, just as Aron had, but it meant something far different to him. It represented the death from above that he'd fled on the battlefield. The memory scared and shamed him. He considered it an act of cowardice that had cost him his place among his own.

They'd gotten some welcome and needed rest in the cave overnight, but now, they must be on their way.

"We have to go." Aron let out an exasperated sigh. "It's what I've come all this way for. She's the only hope for my brothers, my Da, Sir Gareth."

"Don't know them. Know you. She burn. She eat. You and me."

"No, she won't. I told you, I know her son. She will listen to me, and she will help us."

"She kill us."

"Look, my friend Doubloon didn't kill me. Neither will she." He conveniently left out the fact that Doubloon had, in fact, killed some of Skrunt's people. He knew he would have to come clean with the koz'thar at some point that his friend was the creature of Skrunt's nightmares. Now was not the time.

"Ogre scared." Skrunt pointed at Aron. "Should be scared, too."

"I am…a little," the boy admitted. "But I have something that will help us."

"Magic sword?"

"No."

"Magic helmet?"

"Not that, either."

Skrunt snorted, not impressed. "What?"

"This," Aron said, pulling the amulet from his shirt. His companion's eyes widened as it twinkled in the sunlight.

"Magic necklace." Skrunt looked a little more hopeful.

"Sort of," Aron answered. "It was a gift from my

friend, Doubloon. It will prove to his mother that I know him. When she sees it, she'll listen. She'll understand he's in trouble, and she'll help us."

Skrunt snorted again, clearly skeptical about the plan. Then, he went back to studying the amulet.

"Pretty, though."

"Listen, I'm going. You don't have to. You can stay here, or you can leave. I won't ask you to do this. But I need to do it."

Without another word, Aron left the cave and set off on the road that would soon begin winding up Skyclaw Mountain. At least, he hoped so. Skrunt watched for a few minutes, then made a decision. He scrambled to follow.

"Go back now." Skrunt was thrilled with the turn of events that had left his human friend frustrated.

"No, we will not." Aron stared up at the rubble that blocked their way. The collapse looked recent, and he suspected it might have happened when the dragon roared. It had shaken the whole mountain, and it could have easily set off a small avalanche. Or maybe, his imagination was exaggerating, and this was just some natural occurrence he was giving an ominous portent.

"We'll just have to go over it."

Skrunt's ears drooped. He shook his head.

"Can you climb up and scout around?" Aron

asked. "You'll make it up there quicker than me. Let me know if you see anything."

The koz'thar stared defiantly, prepared to argue, then he twisted his mouth, so the bottom fangs stuck out at an angle and sighed. He turned and scrambled up the pile of debris. Rocks bounced down and rolled away as he climbed, but the shifting pile beneath his feet didn't seem to bother him. At the top, he walked back and forth along the obstacle.

"What can you see?" Aron asked.

"Nothing. More road other side. That's it."

The boy wasn't sure what he'd expected his companion to find on top of the pile. It was clearly just a collapse, but he'd hoped that maybe it had uncovered some mystical entrance to the dragon's lair. It hadn't.

"Wait." Skrunt waved him up. "See something. Come look."

Aron's ascent of the rubble pile was nowhere near as graceful as his friend's. He lost his footing a few times and once slid about halfway back down before he finally reached the peak. The view was exactly as Skrunt had described. Beyond the blockage, the road continued just as it had before. He looked to the koz'thar, who was motioning for him to walk out to the end of the debris. The pile thinned and was even more loose out there. With every step, he expected it to give away beneath his feet and send him sliding back down to the road, possibly with a ton of rocks coming down on top of him. Finally, though, he stood next to Skrunt.

"What did you want me to see?"

His companion pointed upward. At first, Aron didn't see anything. Then, he looked higher. There, well above them, on the side of Skyclaw Mountain, stood a huge opening in the rock face. He studied it carefully. From what he could see, the road didn't go nearly that far up the mountain. Unless you could fly, there was only one way to get there, and it was steep and treacherous. But there was almost no doubt in his mind that this was their destination. Determined, he walked back across the rubble and began to climb.

A strong hand from above grabbed his flailing right arm, sharp fingers biting into his wrist painfully.

Twenty-Eight

Aron decided quickly that his backpack had to go. He needed to eliminate extra weight, so only about ten or fifteen feet up, he shrugged out of it and tossed it back to the rubble below. He'd been loath to let go of his few possessions, but he knew that it would only slow him down and possibly send him tumbling to his death. The danger was so serious that he briefly considered leaving his sword, too, but he couldn't bring himself to do that. He knew it wouldn't be any use against the dragon if she were to attack, but the gift from Devan meant enough to him that he couldn't let it go.

As usual, Skrunt was far more agile than Aron, and he quickly passed him by, scrambling up the side of the mountain, seemingly without a care or fear. The boy couldn't say the same. He made the mistake of looking down when he'd been fifty or sixty feet up. A bout of dizziness overtook him, and he almost fell. From that point on, his gaze was only up, focusing on the goal.

From the ground, he'd feared that it would be a mostly sheer climb, and he knew now if that had been the case, he would never have made it. Some areas were almost straight up, but there were also ledges along the way, almost terraces, where they could move a little more easily. It was still treacherous, and a slip could mean a much quicker trip back down the mountain than he wanted to think about.

At the edge of one of the sheer drops, he was nearly lost. As always, he moved very slowly and deliberately, testing each hand and foot hold before putting weight on it. Just as he pulled his right hand away to find the next hold, his right foot slipped off the rock he was perched on. He swung precariously, trying to keep calm and focus on getting a hold on the wall again. A strong hand from above grabbed his flailing right arm, sharp fingers biting into his wrist painfully. Very slowly, Skrunt pulled him back toward the rock face and up to the ledge where the koz'thar waited.

Aron rolled onto his back and closed his eyes as he reached the solid ground, giving thanks for his good fortune. After a few minutes, he rolled to his side and opened his eyes, looking at the companion who saved him. Skrunt stared at him with concerned eyes.

"Thank you. You saved me."

"What friends do." The koz'thar repeated his own words back to him.

"I guess it is."

The sun was growing low behind them, and darkness was beginning to overtake the peak. The grueling climb had taken most of the afternoon. Aron peered up at the cave and realized they'd made more progress than he thought. The entrance was no more than another seventy or eighty feet above them, but the space between here and there would be the toughest climb of the journey. There were no more terraces, and while the slope was not straight up, the face looked smoother, with fewer handholds. He wished, not for the first time, that he'd retrieved the rope he used to tie up the goblin.

Aron's first instinct after a short rest was to begin climbing again. They were so close. He could make it tonight and be done with this quest. But as he stared at the darkening skies, he realized that attempting to climb this section by moonlight was inviting disaster. Skrunt looked relieved when he announced, finally, that they would sleep there for the night.

The boy inspected their surroundings, but there wasn't much to work with. The ledge was essentially all the hard, reddish-gray stone of the mountain. His pack with the blanket, flint, and tinder was far below, not that there was anything here to fuel a fire. It was going to be a long, cold, uncomfortable night.

THE BOY SLEPT FITFULLY and rose with the dawn. He'd halfway hoped the dragon would emerge from her lair in the night and discover them. Then, he wouldn't have to face the climb before them. No such luck. That also put doubt into his mind for the first time. He knew the dragon was there. He'd heard her roar back at the ogre, and the sound was unmistakable. Nothing else could have made that terrifying shriek. But what if this wasn't the entrance to her lair, after all? What if they'd risked their lives climbing up here for nothing? He couldn't think like that. He had to be right.

He expected they would cover the eighty feet or so to the cavern opening fairly quickly, but the climb was even more difficult than it looked from below. Skrunt, of course, had a much easier time of it. He'd been perched just below the ledge for about fifteen minutes before Aron finally pulled himself up on the same level.

They locked eyes, and the koz'thar gave him one last pleading look.

"Can go back."

"No, we can't." Aron fought the temptation to look down, remembering what had happened last time from a much lower height. Even if he wanted to retreat, they couldn't go that way. "We're here. We have to go in."

"You first," Skrunt said, still seeming to hold out hope Aron would change his mind.

He didn't. This was what he'd come all this way for. He heaved himself up over the ledge and instead of resting, as had been their habit, he rolled to his feet warily, scanning the area. The cavern roof loomed high above. The opening was massive, as tall as two or three Doubloons and at least that wide as well.

Aron turned back to help his friend over the ledge, but as usual, Skrunt needed no assistance. He hopped up much more gracefully than the boy had managed.

Aron scanned the area for any sign that might indicate a dragon lived here, but he saw nothing but cold, hard stone. Despite the size of the cave mouth, the farthest reaches were still obscured in inky blackness. He didn't look forward to walking into that darkness, but it was the only way they could move. There was no going back.

Skrunt offered one last questioning look, but Aron shook his head. With a deep breath, he took a step into the cavern. The companions were pulled up short before they even left the light of the entrance by a deafening voice in their heads.

You are brave thieves; I will give you that. But you will soon be dead ones as well.

Twenty-Nine

Glowing eyes appeared in the gloom of the cavern as the dragon slowly emerged. Aron had thought Doubloon was huge. He stood, stunned, as the immense head and neck of his friend's mother snaked out of the darkness and into the light. Like her son, she had twisted horns that swept back from her head and a row of spikes rising from her neck. They were fully extended to their most deadly position. Her scales glimmered like his friend's, but they were of a brilliant platinum. They shone such that it seemed to Aron that he should be able to see his reflection in them.

The boy and his companion were rooted to the spot in a mixture of awe and terror at the sight of the great creature who had roamed the world for millennia but had been seen by only a few.

As her head came into full view, her mouth split

open in a horrifying mockery of a smile, revealing sharp and shining teeth that were easily larger than Aron. Her forked red tongue flickered out in their direction, and she breathed in deeply.

That broke the spell. The boy knew what came next, and he couldn't let that happen.

"We are not thieves! I swear!" he yelled. "We've come for your help."

He cringed away, expecting death, but the dreaded fire didn't come. Instead, she looked at him curiously.

What help could a human child and a... she glanced to Skrunt with a look of disgust, *goblin think one such as I would be willing to give them? And what would they have to offer in return?*

"It's not for us," Aron said quickly, while the dragon was still willing to talk. "Well, it's partially for me, but mainly for your son. Doubloon is in trouble."

She appeared confused for a moment. Then, Aron heard the icy voice in his head again.

Ah, son. You mean my wyrmling. I know of no creature called a Doubloon, and I assure you that if my wyrmling were in trouble, I would be aware of it. Enough of your lies.

"There's magic involved. He told me about the connection dragons have with their dams and sires, but a wizard is blocking it. That's why you can't sense his danger."

I do not believe you, little human. This sounds like a tall tale to save your miserable lives.

Aron took an involuntary step back toward the ledge as the dragon pulled the rest of her body out of the darkness, standing before them in her full glory. He'd never imagined a creature so immense. She filled the cavern that would hold several dragons the size of Doubloon with little room to spare. Her tail flicked in agitation as she considered them.

Now, should I burn you or eat you? Certainly, the goblin would not be a fit meal, but you, little human…

Her head snaked down slowly until her nose almost touched his chest. Her hot, damp breath washed over him, making him take another involuntary step backward. He felt the long fall to his death at his back and wondered for a second which end would be better, the fall or being eaten by a dragon.

He reached into the neck of his shirt and fumbled with the amulet, struggling with shaking hands to hold it out in front of him. On seeing it, the dragon pulled back to her full height, but instead of softening her tone, as he expected, she became enraged.

You should not have that! You say you are no thief, but you have surely stolen that jewel. My wyrmling would not part with it willingly. What have you done to him, human?

The voice in his head rattled his skull in its anger, and Aron found it hard to think. He knew he had to talk fast.

"N-nothing. Doubloon is my friend."

Again, I know of no creature called Doubloon, nor do I care about it.

"S-sorry. That's what I call him because he said I wouldn't be able to pronounce his name. H-he agreed to it, even liked it, I think."

Even if that is true, which I doubt, he would not have given you that. You do not know what it is that you hold.

"I do. He told me about it. The thing that looks like a red jewel is a scale from his Da, um, his sire, who was killed by…"

Yes, go on.

"Um…humans," Aron said sheepishly.

Which is why he would never entrust it to a human. I taught him better. You have clearly stolen it.

"I swear I didn't. It was a gift, so that I could call on him if I got in trouble."

Did he tell you, then, what happened to the last human to hold that trinket?

"Uh…no. I had no idea that he'd given it to a human before."

Oh, no, child. The last human to hold that was one of the men who killed my mate, my wyrmling's sire. The man took one of his scales and had it encased in gold and put on a chain as a trophy. I took it back.

The frigid venom in the last statement sent a shiver through Aron.

I took back all of their trophies and more. Much more.

The menace that accompanied her statement made him feel very small and inconsequential. But another tactic occurred to him. Maybe he could use her hatred of humans in his favor.

"It's a human who has captured Doubloon—a wizard. He holds him in an enchanted net. It's too strong for him to tear apart, and it doesn't allow him to use magic or talk to me in my head like you're doing now. He also believes it might keep you from sensing he is in danger."

I suppose you expect me to believe this wizard intends to slay my wyrmling?

"No. Not yet anyway. He wants to enslave him, use him as a weapon."

This human attempts to make my wyrmling serve him?

The uncontrolled rage in the voice almost dropped Aron to his knees. All he could do was nod weakly. Then, the oppressive anger disappeared.

I do not believe this lie. My wyrmling would not allow himself to be captured. You are hoping that I will fly off to save him, so you can sneak into my lair and make off with my treasures.

"No, no. We need to travel with you to save him."

And why would I need a human boy and a goblin to save my wyrmling? What can you possibly do to help?

"The wizard has captured my family and friends as well. We need to save them, too."

Ah, so that is it. You want me to do your dirty work. You wish me to attack this wizard, so you can free your people, so you have concocted this story about my wyrmling in an attempt to deceive me. Know that I cannot be deceived.

"It's no lie. Doubloon…your wyrmling…is in trouble. And…I owe him."

She tilted her head, giving him an appraising look.

Why is it that you believe you owe him?

Aron didn't want to share what he was about to reveal to the angry dragon. He wasn't sure how she would take it. She might burn him on the spot for it. But he had to convince her he was telling the truth.

"It's…uh…kind of my fault he got captured…" He paused, unsure how to continue.

Go on.

"Well, I convinced him to help my village, which was being attacked by goblins. He saved it, but that's… uh…how the wizard found out he existed."

You expect me to believe this story when you travel here with a goblin? Perhaps you are in league with this wizard.

"Skrunt isn't like the others. He left their army. I met him on the way here, and I wouldn't have made it without him."

It is unlike a goblin to help with no benefit to himself. Another poor lie.

"But that's exactly what he's done. Just like Doubloon did. I had nothing to offer your wyrmling but my friendship, and he was willing to risk his life for that. It's my fault he's a prisoner. You have to help him. You're the only one who can."

Though he tried to remain brave in the face of the great dragon, tears began to roll down his face. He'd come all this way to help his friend, to help his family, and she refused to believe him. It was all a waste, hopeless. He dropped to his knees, sobbing. Skrunt scooted over next to him and put a tentative arm around his shoulder. Then, the koz'thar, who had cowered through the whole meeting and believed himself to be a coward, looked up defiantly into the face of the towering, platinum dragon.

"No like you," he said. "Make Aron cry. Aron good friend. To me. To Doubloon. You mean. No need you. Aron and Skrunt save friends without you."

If it were possible for a dragon to look shocked, this one did. She stared down at the defiant koz'thar, and the tiny creature didn't cower. He appeared ready to fight her by himself.

Hmm. I wonder now what kind of human could inspire such loyalty in a lowly goblin.

On hearing that, Aron stood again, gaining strength from his friend's defense. He met the dragon's eyes with a steady gaze.

"He is koz'thar, not a goblin, and he is not lowly. He's more honorable than many humans I've known, and perhaps more honorable than one dragon I've met."

The great beast drew back in obvious surprise. Then, she chuckled and sighed.

My wyrmling was always soft when it came to lesser creatures. Very well, I will hear your tale. Tell me from the beginning.

Thirty

Aron recounted the whole story of the last two years, starting with his flight from Lanfield, how he blundered into Doubloon's cave in the mountains, and how his friend had most likely saved his life. He shared the tale of the battle at his village, and the great, shining dragon looked proud as he told of how her wyrmling had singlehandedly routed the giant army of monsters and men.

Skrunt trembled and whimpered at that part of the tale, staring at his new friend with frightened eyes as he made the connection. Aron squeezed his shoulder with a comforting hand, longing to explain, but it would have to wait. He needed to keep the dragon's attention.

He told her about the abduction of his brothers and how he'd used the amulet to call Doubloon for help. He was even honest about how he'd urged the dragon to attack the camp in daylight against his own advice, even though he feared her reaction to that news. She did, indeed, narrow her eyes to slits, but she remained silent. He left nothing out because he needed her to believe him, needed her to agree to help.

He finished the story with the flight from the ogre and how they'd located her with her response to the monster's roar. When he was finished, Aron looked up at the shining dragon hopefully.

"Hmm," she said, speaking aloud for the first time. Her voice was clear and musical, as beautiful as her platinum scales and completely unlike the fearsome visage. "I wondered what had tempted that creature into my domain. He knows better than to intrude here. Perhaps, I should have let him eat you."

Aron sagged at her cold tone. It seemed she still didn't believe him. He opened his mouth to plead his case again, but she cut him off.

"Still, your story bears the feel of truth. You were honest, even when you knew that what you were saying might anger me. I do not like that you led my wyrmling into danger with your foolishness, but I appreciate your bravery in telling the truth," she paused, "and in what you faced to find me in order to help him, even if it was for partially selfish reasons."

Silence fell in the cavern, so encompassing that Aron thought his heartbeat sounded abnormally loud in the void. The dragon took several minutes to decide what she would do.

"Very well. I believe you, which means that I must

fly to the aid of my wyrmling. What can you tell me of his human wizard?"

"Not much," Aron answered truthfully. "I've never even seen him. He wants Doubloon to fight for him, and his magic is apparently strong enough to create a net that can hold a dragon."

Skrunt spoke up.

"Powerful. Proud. Treat koz'thar good. Unless make him angry." He shuddered in fear. "Don't make angry."

"How do you know so much about the wizard?" The dragon turned her attention fully onto Skrunt, and the bravery the koz'thar had shown while defending Aron drained from him. He drooped and stared at the stone beneath his feet.

"Served him. He promise koz'thar safe home if we help. All followed."

"And what are the…koz'thar…helping him with?" The dragon seemed to ponder this new word as she said it for the first time.

"Hates human king. Big hate. King's father…" Skrunt screwed up his face, thinking hard. "What word? Not know what means. Eggsle? No. Ecksel. Not it."

He considered each word as he said it and shook his head in frustration. Then, his eyes lit. "Exile. That word. King's father exile him. Wants revenge. Friends don't like king, either."

"Friends?" Aron interrupted. "There are more wizards?"

Skrunt shook his head.

"Other humans. Two. Not nice. No like koz'thar at all. Mean to us."

The dragon took control of the conversation again. "What kind of magic have you seen this wizard use?"

"Lots. Make big winds. Set fires. Lightning."

Then, the small creature shivered and looked terrified as he remembered something. His face twisted. "Talk in your head. Not like you. Feels bad. Like worm in brain. Make see things. He sees, too."

Skrunt looked panicked. He drew in on himself, wrapping his arms tightly around his body and rocking back and forth. "Can't go back. He see Skrunt run. He punish. Hurt. Hurt bad."

It was Aron's turn to comfort his friend now. He knelt next to the koz'thar and wrapped an arm around him, pulling him close.

"It's OK. We won't let him hurt you, will we?" He looked up to the dragon. She sniffed.

"I care not what he does to you, but let him try to get in my head, and he will know what true pain and suffering means. Though he may well learn that anyway for what he has done to my wyrmling."

"Does that mean you're going to help us?" Aron asked hopefully.

"No. It means I am going to help my wyrmling. Should you touch any of my treasures while I am gone, you will know the same pain and suffering as the wizard."

"You have to take us with you," Aron demanded.

"Do I now?" The edge of anger came back into the dragon's voice, and the boy knew he had to think quickly.

"We know where the wizard's army is," he said. "We can get you there faster, so you don't have to waste any time searching. And Skrunt has been among the army. He'll know what we're looking at and can help you plan your attack."

"I need no help in attacking a ragged mob of humans and goblins," she said coldly, but then she tilted her head, considering. "Still, there is some truth to what you say. Very well, you may go with me."

Aron walked over to the side of the dragon and stood there expectantly.

"What are you doing?" she asked.

"Waiting for you to put down your wing, so I can climb on. It's how I get on Doubloon's back."

The boy couldn't have imagined a dragon being horrified before that moment, but there she was. A low growl came almost unbidden from her throat.

"Absolutely not! No human is going to ride me like a common beast of burden, and certainly no goblin."

She sniffed and turned her head away from them.

"How will we travel then?" Aron asked. "We can't fly, and we definitely can't travel as fast as you across the mountains. It took us weeks to get here."

The dragon sighed.

"Wait here. I will return shortly."

With that, she stepped past them to the mouth of the cavern and launched herself out across the drop that Aron and Skrunt had climbed to get there. She plummeted out of their sight for a second, then snapped her wings open and soared into the sky, wheeling and sailing gracefully out of their sight to the east. Her flight made Doubloon look clumsy in comparison, and for the first time, Aron began to realize that he and his friend might be more alike than he thought.

Thirty-One

A large farm cart thudded down on the ledge at the front of the cavern, and the dragon landed closely behind it. Aron winced at the sight of it, knowing that some farmer was now missing a valuable piece of equipment. He secretly hoped she had stolen it from Ebbner and Oma but figured it came from somewhere much closer.

"Get in the cart," the dragon said. "Then, you will show me where to find my wyrmling."

As he made his way to where the wagon had landed, Aron thought that he couldn't just keep calling her dragon or Doubloon's mother. He decided he needed to give his friend's dam a name that he could pronounce. What should he propose, though? He certainly didn't want to offend her. She was much larger than his friend, so what was larger than a doubloon?

"If we're going to be traveling together, I need something to call you," he said hesitantly. "Would the name Ingot be OK with you?"

"You may call me whatever you wish, child. I will never answer to it. My wyrmling may be soft and sentimental, but I am not. I know the treachery of humans all too well. We are not friends. Once he is safe, our business is done."

Aron sighed and crawled into the cart. Skrunt scrambled over the side behind him.

"She not like very much."

"No, she doesn't. But she may change her mind."

"Not likely," said the icy voice from above. Then, two great talons locked onto the wagon, and the wind blew Aron's hair back as she launched them into the sky.

FLYING in the cart was quite different from being tied into a harness on Doubloon's shoulders. Aron scooted as close to the center as he could and spent most of his time staring at the worn wood of the floor. The ride induced sickness, and occasionally, Ingot would forget she had passengers and take a turn that tilted the wagon dizzyingly. She seemed annoyed at their cries when that happened.

"I will not drop you, as much as I might like to," she told them. That didn't make Aron feel any better.

Skrunt fared far worse. Unlike Aron, the poor koz'thar had never been in the air. He curled up in a ball, rocking back and forth and shivering for most of the flight. The boy tried to comfort him, but it was no use.

"Koz'thar not meant fly," was all he would say, then go back to his rocking.

Aron was stunned at just how fast they traveled. Ingot flew on the north side of the mountains and high up to avoid detection. The freezing cold and thin air wasn't helping the mood of her passengers, but at least the flight would be relatively short. At the speed the dragon was moving, they appeared to be covering the ground it took him weeks to traverse in a single day.

Despite the promise he'd made to Ingot, he was concerned that he wouldn't actually be able to lead her back to the wizard's camp. He'd never seen the territory from the sky and had no idea where they were, not that he wanted to look down from the dizzying heights anyway. When they settled to the ground for the night, Aron thought they should be near, but he really had no idea. As they descended, he scanned for any recognizable landmark from his travels, but one mountainside full of rocks looked much like any other.

"How far to the enemy camp where my wyrmling is being held?" Ingot demanded.

"We're close," Aron said. "Maybe a few more hours."

He prayed they would be able to spot the fires of

the camp from the sky, and the dragon wouldn't discover his fib.

"I must rest," she said. "We will leave again in a few hours. I care not what you and the goblin do, but do not stray far. If you are not here when I am ready to go, I will leave without you."

Aron nodded his understanding. It wasn't like he and Skrunt had anywhere to go. They might scout around for something to eat, but options were limited. The stolen bow had been broken and left behind, and his snares were still in his pack on the side of Skyclaw Mountain, along with his flint to start a fire. If they found something, they might convince Ingot to give them fire, but Aron didn't want to press his luck by disturbing her. Instead, they huddled and slept near the dragon.

He felt as if he'd barely been asleep when Ingot woke them with a loud word. They climbed groggily back into the cart and were off again on their westward flight under the moonlight. The dragon flew lower under cover of darkness, less concerned about being seen from the ground. It was nearing dawn when they finally spotted lights in the distance.

Is this the camp? Ingot asked, using the voice in his head again.

"I think it may be. Get us closer."

As they neared the fires, Aron realized his mistake. There were buildings below, and they looked very familiar. He'd seen them from Doubloon's back. They were approaching his village. He took a deep breath and prepared himself to deliver the bad news.

"This isn't it. This is my village. We've gone too far. I must have missed it in the dark."

You told me that you knew where this wizard's army is, child.

"I did," he said quickly. "I do. It's back to the east on the edge of the mountains. An afternoon and a morning's flight for Doubloon, but you move much faster. We can probably make it in a few hours."

The dragon said nothing more, only circled and headed back the way they'd come. The boy could still feel her displeasure. Despite the discomfort it caused him, he sat at the edge of the cart, keeping an eye out for the camp. Ingot flew lower since there was little danger of being seen in this area. That helped.

After about two-and-a-half hours of travel, Aron breathed a sigh of relief when he spotted a familiar landmark—the outcropping from which he and Doubloon had studied the camp.

"It's just ahead." He was worried. He should be able to see the tents from here, and he could not. As they got closer, he could see evidence of where the camp had been, but it was only an empty field now, filled with ruts and the remnants of fires. Ingot landed in the middle of it.

"Where is my wyrmling? Where is this wizard?" she asked.

"They were here. But my trip over the mountains to find you took weeks. They must have moved."

Luckily, the trail was not hard to find. An army of goblins and men left quite the track in their wake. They quickly spotted the ruts leading north and were on the hunt again.

By mid-morning, they spotted the tendrils of smoke rising in the distance. Ingot slowed and soared higher into the clouds, so she wouldn't be seen as she surveyed the scene. Aron could make out very little from that height, but what he couldn't miss was the silhouette of his friend in the middle of the camp. He appeared to still be restrained. Ingot realized what she was seeing at the same time he did. She gave a great growl and pulled up, hovering in the air. Aron recognized the move as the same one Doubloon made when preparing to dive.

"Stop! Wait!" he yelled.

She paused. *Why should I?*

"It could be a trap," Aron answered. "Just like for Doubloon."

I will not be as foolish as my wyrmling.

"My family is in there, too," he pleaded. "If you just dive in and destroy everything, they could be hurt. We need to get them out first."

What do I care for humans? My wyrmling is in trouble. That is all that matters.

"He's safe for now, and he cares about us. He wouldn't want to see my Da or my brothers get hurt, either. He saved us, after all. He'll be mad at you if they are."

He has been angry with me before. I care not. He will be free.

"Without us, you wouldn't know he's in danger. You owe us that much, at least."

Understand this. I owe you nothing. However, I will consider your assistance. How do you propose to free your humans?

"I have a plan," he said. In fact, he'd been thinking about it throughout the whole flight. He gave a side-ways, nervous glance to Skrunt. "But one of us is not going to like it."

"Hold," the guard commanded as they came near. "What do we have here?"

Thirty-Two

"NO!" Skrunt crossed his arms and glared at Aron defiantly, just as he had on Skyclaw Mountain. The little koz'thar reminded him of one of his younger brothers when they were upset.

"I'm open to any better ideas you have," the boy said. "But this is the only way I can think of."

"Won't go back. Wizard punish."

"He'll never even know you're there. I just need you to get me in, then you can leave and come back here."

"No," the koz'thar said firmly.

"Listen, there has to be someone in there you want to save. If Ingot attacks, everyone who is still there is in danger. Don't you have friends or family you'd like to get out?"

Skrunt considered for a moment, then he drooped. "Grottma," he whispered.

"Your mother is in there?"

Skrunt nodded.

"You can get her out, just like I can get my Da and brothers out."

The koz'thar still looked uncertain.

The dragon, who had been watching their drama from a short distance away, finally spoke, "Whatever you two are going to do, you had best decide soon. Once darkness falls, nothing will stop me from razing the camp to the ground."

Aron turned back to Skrunt, trying to project a confidence that he didn't feel himself. "Just trust me."

AS THEY APPROACHED THE CAMP, Aron recognized one of the guards. Luckily, it was the more reasonable of the two men he'd passed when he'd disguised himself to try to free Doubloon. The other might have been a problem.

They dusted off Skrunt's black robe and tried to make the tattered thing look as presentable as possible. Then, the koz'thar loosely tied Aron's hands behind his back with a piece of hemp rope that had been attached to the cart. The boy held them together, but it would be an easy thing to drop the rope and free them. He wasn't able to bring his sword for obvious reasons, but his knife was tucked into his boot and covered by his pants. It bit uncomfortably into his leg, but it was the best he could do. He left the amulet in Ingot's care. He hated to part with it, but he knew it would likely get taken in the camp.

"Hold," the guard commanded as they came near. "What do we have here?"

"Prisoner," Skrunt said.

The man stared long and hard at the koz'thar. "Do I know you?"

"They all look the same," said the other guard, a bored expression on his face. "They're all ugly. How can you tell?"

"Where did you capture this prisoner?"

"Village," Skrunt said. "Wizard send. Weeks ago. Had to find. Camp moved. Special prisoner. Wizard want. Put with others."

"Why does he want this kid?"

Skrunt shrugged. "Something about dragon. Skrunt sent…find."

Aron felt great pride in his friend. He knew just how terrified the koz'thar was, but he seemed unconcerned as he talked to the guards. The first one turned his attention to the boy.

"What do you have to say for yourself, boy? This true?"

Aron looked straight ahead and said nothing.

"Speak up, boy. This little bugger really capture you in a village?"

Aron dropped his gaze to the ground and nodded slightly.

The guard guffawed. "Don't see how valuable you can be if you can't get away from a runt like this."

Skrunt drew himself up to his full, unimpressive height and glared at the guard. "Important prisoner," he said with authority. "Wizard angry if delayed."

The guard shook his head and waved them through lazily. "Yeah, yeah. Take him and put him with the rest."

Aron breathed a sigh of relief as they passed into the camp, but it was short-lived. They were already drawing stares and mutters, and he wanted as little attention as possible. There was nothing to be done about it. The news of a human prisoner being escorted was going to spread. He just hoped word didn't get to the wizard.

"They're in the second largest tent over there. Hand me over to the koz'thar guards and go get your mother out." Aron glanced up at the sun briefly. It was much lower than he would have liked. "We only have a couple of hours left."

They repeated the ruse at the entrance to the tent. The koz'thar were a bit more suspicious than the human guards and had more questions for Skrunt. Aron couldn't understand their conversation, which was in their own guttural language, but his friend put on a haughty, indignant tone with them until they relented. Aron thought he'd make a good actor.

Finally, one of the guards grabbed the boy roughly and dragged him inside the tent. His heart soared almost as soon as he was through the flap. He'd expected to see them in chains, but instead, he found his Da, his brothers, and Sir Gareth sitting around a table in the middle of the tent, almost as if they were in the kitchen at home. They all appeared unharmed, and they were stunned to see him walk in. Apparently, the wizard had believed Doubloon's threats about keeping them safe.

"Aron!" his father yelled and rose from the table to approach him. The koz'thar guard stepped between them and stopped him with a snarl. A small crackle of electricity sparked on the creature's hand, and his Da stepped back.

The one who had threatened his father motioned to another guard and said something in their language. The second one came up, cut the rope that held Aron's hands, not seeming to notice how loosely it was tied, and began to pat him down. He held his breath. Much of the plan depended on this. He was relieved that the goblin began at his shoulders instead of his feet. If they'd found the knife first, that would be a problem.

The guard stopped at his pocket, feeling a lump. He shoved his hand roughly into Aron's pocket, pulling out the jar of calmthorn cream that he'd left there on purpose. He examined it, opened the container, and sniffed it. He shoved it into the boy's face.

"What this?"

"Nothing important," Aron answered, his eyes

darting from side to side. He did his best to look nervous like he was lying.

"He lie," the first guard said.

"What this?" the second asked again, more forcefully. Aron didn't answer. The first guard turned and raised his hand toward the boy, the energy once again crackling from his fingertips.

"Answer," the creature said.

"It's nothing," Aron said again. The magic worried him, but he had to make them believe he was lying. The first koz'thar placed his hand on the boy's chest. He heard a pop, and an acrid smell filled the air. He was thrown backward as waves of pain shot through him. It took a minute or so for it to pass, and that was enough for him to know he didn't want to feel it again.

"Tell truth." The guard walked toward him, the sparks crackling again.

"Tell him, son," his father pleaded. "Whatever it is, tell him."

The koz'thar reached out again, leaning down toward Aron.

"OK. OK." Aron held up a hand, staving off the magical attack. "It's an ointment of power."

"What do?"

"It makes your magic stronger." He sagged, trying to appear defeated. "The more you rub on, the stronger your magic will be."

"More rub, more magic?"

Aron nodded.

The first guard snatched the jar and dipped a finger into it. He sniffed the ointment, then dabbed a little on his arm. He waited a moment to see if anything would happen. When it didn't, he slathered the cream all over his arms.

"Have all power now," he said, sparking the magic on his fingers again. It was the same as before, but the koz'thar looked at it in satisfaction.

"Me now." The second guard snatched the jar back and also put a large amount of the cream on himself. A third guard, who had stayed near the entrance, looked in. After a quick conversation, he entered and took the container. Aron tried to look miserable as they covered themselves in calmthorn, even though he was grinning like an idiot inside. It actually worked. Now, he only had to hope that the herb had the same effect on them as it did on humans.

The first guard shoved Aron toward the others at the table. He stumbled and was caught in a big hug by his father. His brothers soon joined in. Then, he looked over to Sir Gareth, who remained stern-faced.

"What do you think you're doing here?" he asked.

"Getting us all out," Aron said quietly.

Thirty-Three

"Just how do you intend to do that?" Gareth asked.

Aron cut his eyes to the three koz'thar guards who were talking excitedly among themselves. "Give it a minute."

"I take it, the ointment doesn't really enhance magical powers?"

The boy grinned as the guards continued to show off their "improved" powers to each other. In a few minutes, they had forgotten their prisoners completely. Apparently, the calmthorn did have a similar effect on them as humans. Aron knew what they were now feeling a great sense of satisfaction and contentment. As much as they'd slathered on, he wasn't entirely sure what the full effects would be. Oma had always warned him to only use a small amount. He honestly wasn't sure if that was because of the potential effects or simply because she was afraid that he'd notice them.

At any rate, the koz'thar were blissfully unaware of anything but their perceived more powerful spells. From what Aron could see, even the strongest of the three had barely an ounce of power.

"Are there any stronger than these?"

His father shook his head. "Never believed magic existed, much less that goblins could use it. But no, the strongest ones seem to have just a little bit, but it's enough to put a wallop on you."

Aron could confirm that much. The jolt from the guard had been agonizing in the moment but seemed to have no long-term ill effects. A couple of them at the same time, though? Who could say? They'd have to be careful to execute the next part of the plan.

He was trying to figure out how they would take out the guards when he noticed that, as time went on, they became more and more excited. They were animated as they showed off their prowess, and though Aron couldn't understand what they were saying, he could interpret their tone. It seemed there was some rising annoyance and disagreement, perhaps about who was stronger.

Finally, the guard who had attacked Aron had enough. He sparked his power and slapped one of the others in the chest with it. That strange smell, a flash, and the second koz'thar was on the ground, rolling in agony. The third guard, the one who had come from the door, turned to his companion and decked him, not with magic, but with a balled-up fist. As the two tied into it, Gareth made his move. They didn't even notice the knight coming toward them until he had them both by the neck and cracked their skulls together. They fell limply to the ground. The third was just recovering and struggling to get up when he caught Sir Gareth's boot in the face and went back down.

The knight turned to them and gave his squire an approving nod.

"Well done. Now, do you have a plan to get us out of a camp with dozens of those and human soldiers, too?"

Aron smiled again, taking pride in both the approval of his mentor and the fact that he did, indeed, have a plan...sort of. He pulled his knife from his boot and crossed to the back of the tent, where he thrust it through the fabric and cut a slit. He cracked it open and peered out. Light was fading fast, and the sky had already begun to darken.

"We need to hurry," he said. "We have to be out of here before the sun sets. Things are going to get ugly then."

"What..." Gareth started to ask, but Aron cut him off, drawing a look of ire from the knight.

"I'll tell you on the way, but we need to go now." With that, he ducked through the gash in the tent and was off.

"So, you traveled across the mountains, found your dragon friend's mother, and convinced her to come here and free us?" Gareth shook his head. Aron had told them the full story as they moved through the shadows, trying to skirt the camp without being seen.

"Well, she came to free Doubloon. I had to convince her to give me time to come in and get everyone out. She doesn't like humans much and would just as soon burn us as the goblins and wizard."

"Great," the knight said sarcastically. "Not that I'm unhappy to be out of there, but that was very foolish. You should have gone to Commander Kyle or at least gotten some of the other knights from the patrols to travel with you."

"Yeah, Doubloon told me that, too. But that would have taken much longer. I didn't know what the wizard intended to do with any of you."

"So far, not much," his father said. "We were treated fairly well. He kept us under guard, always with a few of those goblins with the magic nearby."

"Koz'thar," Aron corrected.

"What?"

"Never mind. I'll explain later."

"Anyway, Gareth and I attempted to fight our way out a few times early on, but once you get hit with that spark magic once or twice, you learn to bide your time.

After a while, we realized they weren't really that interested in us."

"The wizard is using you to try to convince Doubloon to join his army," Aron said. "He told me he'd make it clear that if you were harmed, there was no chance he'd ever join them."

"Guess we owe him for that."

"Speaking of which," Gareth interrupted, "where is this other dragon, and how far do we have to go to find her?"

As if on cue, a fireball exploded in the middle of the camp, and Ingot came shrieking out of the darkening sky. The sound of her cries sent a shock wave across the land, and even Aron felt rooted to the spot in terror for a moment as fear of the dragon washed over him. As soon as the sound faded, the wizard's army burst into chaos, with men and goblins running and screaming. Another gout of flame struck the tents of the human army, setting most of them ablaze.

Aron was the first in the group to break free of the spell.

"I think she found us." He grabbed Eli, the smallest of his brothers, and hoisted him onto his shoulders. "We need to get out of here. She will destroy everything."

Shaking himself from the trance, his father grabbed Caleb, and the whole group began to dash for the woods. Another scream from the dragon brought them up short. Aron turned to see her dive into the center of the camp, where Doubloon lay on a giant cart, wrapped tight in the magical net that had captured him. He returned the cry as she snatched the webbing up in her rear talons and jerked it away from her wyrmling. Her flight faltered for just a second as she lifted the net, perhaps an effect of its magic, but she quickly tossed it to the ground and righted herself. Then, she unleashed her fury.

If Aron thought Doubloon had been scary defending the village, his rage paled in comparison to his mother. Ingot became vengeance incarnate. Each shriek froze every enemy on the battlefield in terror, and she burned them where they stood. The boy looked away from the carnage. As much as he hated the humans and koz'thar who had captured and held his family and friends, her wrath was difficult to watch, especially as he thought about Skrunt.

As she released another terrifying cry, a bolt of blue lightning struck the shining dragon from below. She tumbled in the air at the impact, turning the fall into a roll and rising again, looking for the source of the attack. Aron got his first real glimpse of the wizard then. He stood in front of the largest tent in heavy black robes, his white hair whipping in the wind from the dragon's wings. Though he seemed miniscule compared to his opponent, he gave not an inch to her.

"You are the wizard who would enslave my wyrmling?" Ingot's voice boomed over the battlefield. Her opponent did not respond. Instead, he pointed his staff toward her and released another bolt of lightning.

The dragon easily dodged the attack and unleashed a blast of fire that engulfed the wizard, incinerating him. It spread beyond where he stood, sending his big, fancy tent up in flames as well. That was that, Aron thought. The magician was dead. Then, the man strode out of the inferno and fired another blast at Ingot. She had clearly thought the same as the boy, that the battle was over. She was taken completely by surprise. The bolt hit her squarely in the chest and sent her spinning backward.

When she recovered, she rose higher into the sky, releasing yet another shriek that almost drove Aron to his knees. The cry caused physical pain. Ingot dove at the wizard, who stood his ground. She was only a few yards from him when she unleashed her fire again. He swung the staff toward her. A great explosion shook the earth around the camp, causing the party to stumble, along with everyone else. Dragon flew one way, and the wizard was thrown in the opposite direction. Ingot hit the ground with a great crash and rolled to a stop at the edge of the camp.

The dragon picked herself up and stretched her neck out with a growl. On the other side of the camp, the man who had managed to take her out of the sky used his staff to pull himself to his feet, preparing for another round. Ingot launched herself off the ground, rising above him again, and he held his staff aloft in front of him. Then, a second dragon joined the battle. Doubloon soared upward to hover next to his dam, and though she was nearly twice his size, he looked every bit as fierce. Together, they released another one of those horrifying shrieks and dove in unison. The wizard turned quickly and waved the staff through the air. A circle of blue light appeared in front of him, and he stepped through it.

Thirty-Four

As soon as the wizard disappeared, his control over his army was broken. Men and goblins ran in complete disarray in all directions. Aron and his friends realized they needed to be gone quickly.

Aron hitched Eli back up on his shoulder. "Follow me."

It took them longer to get to where they'd left Ingot than the boy thought it would. They'd had to hide several times as large bands of men or goblins ran past. Sir Gareth had dealt with the few lone stragglers they'd come across, and he now had a sword and a shield. Though they were of poor quality compared to the ones issued by the knights, Gareth used them just as effectively when the group was threatened.

Finally, they reached the spot where he'd left his sword, the only thing that remained of what he'd taken with him. Skrunt was already there. Sir Gareth raised the blade and stalked toward the koz'thar.

"Wait!" Aron shouted. "He's with us."

The knight turned and looked at him, dumbfounded.

"Son, that's a goblin," his father said from behind.

"Koz'thar," Aron corrected again. "They call themselves koz'thar. At least the ones that speak and know magic. I wouldn't have been able to bring the dragon without Skrunt…and he's my friend."

"This is preposterous," Gareth said. "Goblins are evil. You can't trust him."

"Koz'thar," Skrunt said. "And Skrunt not evil."

The knight turned back toward Aron's friend, his jaw dropping.

"He's saved my life, and I've saved his," the boy said. "I trust him as much as I trust you."

Gareth looked back and forth between the two of them and just shook his head. Aron's father looked on the verge of laughter.

"Well, son, I will say that you never cease to amaze me. First, dragons. Now, wizards and good goblins. Whatever crazy dreams you have next, I hope they're for the great wealth of your family."

Aron laughed and hugged his Da and brothers again, taking the moment of calm to greet them properly. Then, something occurred to him. He turned back to Skrunt.

"Did you find your Mum? Your grottma?"

The little creature looked sad, his ears drooping in the way that had become familiar to Aron when his friend was uncomfortable.

"Not come," he said quietly. "Call me disgrace. Said I should trust wizard. Have no family."

The boy crossed the clearing and pulled his friend into a tight hug.

"You're not a disgrace, and you have a family." He turned and waved at the others in the clearing. "You've even got a dragon in it."

A look of fear swept across Skrunt's face at the mention of Doubloon, his nightmare of gold and fire, and his lip quivered a bit. Seeing his discomfort, Aron leaned into him. "It's OK. You'll like him when you get to know him."

His father looked skeptical, but Aron's younger brothers approached the koz'thar tentatively.

"These are my brothers, Caleb and Eli," Aron introduced them. "This is Skrunt."

"Nice to meet you, Skrunt," Caleb said, tentatively extending his hand. The creature's eyes widened, but he returned the gesture, clasping the young boy's hand. Eli followed his brother's lead.

By the time the rustling leaves of the trees announced the arrival of the two dragons, Aron's younger brothers were talking animatedly with Skrunt, asking all kinds of questions as their father watched in bemusement, shaking his head in disbelief every now and then.

Doubloon landed first, and Aron ran to him. The dragon leaned his head down, and the boy latched his arms around his friend's neck, squeezing tightly.

"Well done, little one," Doubloon said. "Even though my dam tells me you did not follow my advice to seek help and almost lost your life."

"It wasn't that bad," Aron said. The dragon and the knight snorted at the same time.

The larger dragon touched down next to her wyrmling and looked at the group with barely disguised disdain. Sir Gareth became suddenly formal, dropping to one knee before her.

"Thank you, milady, for your assistance," he said. "Sir Gareth Rayne at your service."

"I have no need of your services, I assure you," she said coldly.

"Be that as it may, I remain in your debt."

"Indeed. Make no mistake, I was only here for my wyrmling. Thank his pet human there for your lives."

"If I may be so bold, we could use your help when the wizard returns, for he surely will."

"Yes, you could. But you will not have it." She swept her head toward Doubloon. "Unlike this one, I have no interest in the affairs of humans and goblins."

"Koz'thar!" Skrunt said angrily. Ingot swung a hard glare toward him, but he stood his ground. She chuckled.

"Although I must admit, this human and... koz'thar...are quite unlike any others I have ever met."

She extended a talon toward Aron. From the end of it hung Doubloon's amulet, which he had given her for safekeeping. "I believe this is yours."

The boy stared at it, stunned for a moment, before taking it from her and placing it back around his neck. He knew she didn't want him to have it, but she was freely returning it to him.

"Thank you."

"Keep it safe. A gift from the hoard of a dragon, especially one with so much meaning, is a rare and powerful thing. I hope you understand and honor it."

He nodded mutely.

"And now, I believe I have had enough of humans and goblins…" Skrunt stood taller, and Ingot chuckled again, "koz'thar. I will take my leave and return to my mountain. Do not seek me again."

With that, she launched herself gracefully into the air, circling upward lazily until she straightened her path toward the northeast. Doubloon watched her go, sadness in his eyes.

All was silent for a moment, until Aron's stomach growled loudly enough for everyone to hear. They all turned to stare at him, and, slowly, they began to laugh.

"Can we get home now?" he asked. "It's been a long journey, and I can't wait for one of Mum's meals."

As they entered the field where the boy's adventure had begun, the dragon already waited.

Thirty-Five

Though the group was exhausted when they walked through the door of Aron's home, that all drained away at the sight of his mother. She had a cup of water halfway to her mouth when they came in, and it clattered to the kitchen table, spraying liquid everywhere. Aron and his brothers would have gotten a stern talking to for something like that, but she hardly seemed to notice as she jumped up from her seat, tipping the chair over in the process, and ran to greet them. Uncertain who to welcome first, she attempted to hug all of them at the same time, and they ended up in a muddled mass of tears and smiles.

After a few moments, his mother's eyes fell on Skrunt, who had remained back by the door, looking like he'd rather be just about anywhere else. Her gaze flickered over those tattered black robes that marked him as one of the wizard's creatures, and she recoiled, looking around for something she could use as a weapon.

"It's OK, Mum," Aron assured her. "This is Skrunt. He's a friend."

She didn't look convinced, but his Da put a comforting arm around her.

"It's true," he said. "Your boy has quite the story to tell."

He shared the whole tale over dinner a few hours later. Jonas came in from the fields, and his wife Nelly helped Aron's mother fill the table with food for all of them. The whole family was together again, and he thought it might have been the most delicious meal ever. His Mum and brother listened raptly to the story. When it was finished, Jonas clapped Aron on the shoulder; his mother only looked at him incredulously and shook her head.

Once he was back in his own cot, full of his mother's cooking, Aron slept for nearly a full day and night. The reunion of the family had been emotional and added to the exhaustion of the last few weeks. He was soundly asleep as soon as his head hit the pillow. His mother had overcome her uneasiness about Skrunt after hearing how the koz'thar had saved Aron's life. She had found a pallet for him, which was laid out next to the boy's bed. They weren't sure what they were going to do about Skrunt. He likely wouldn't be welcomed in the village, given what they'd been through. But that was a decision that could wait until later.

After lunch on their second day home, Aron and Skrunt joined his father and Sir Gareth on a walk to the edge of the mountains to meet with Doubloon. While the dragon was becoming more comfortable around humans, he still would not willingly show himself in the village. As they entered the field where the boy's adventure had begun, the dragon already waited. He looked pleased to see his friend.

"You look much better," he said, studying Aron. "I am glad. I was concerned."

"I'll be fine," the boy assured him. "A few more days of Mum's cooking and a little more rest, I'll be as good as new."

"Unfortunately, we may not have that luxury," Gareth said.

The knight had been troubled by the information Aron and Skrunt had shared with him over the past few days. It wasn't much, but he'd made them go over it again on the walk.

"The wizard was exiled by King Richard, and now, he wants revenge on King James? And he has other human allies who also hate the king?" Skrunt nodded his agreement, and Gareth looked thoughtful.

"You suspect you know our enemies?" Aron's father asked.

"It lines up with what some of the captives of our last battle told Commander Kyle. Of the wizard, I know little more than what our friend Skrunt has been able to tell us. I had no idea that such a thing existed until a few weeks ago and still wouldn't believe it if I hadn't seen it with my own eyes. If he's truly an exile, someone at court will know who he is. The magician will be a formidable foe, but if I'm correct about his allies, they bring another kind of power to bear. Only two nobles of the court opposed King James's ascension to the throne—Lord Edmund Ashford and Lord Charles Penhurst. Edmund served as King Richard's right hand and felt he had a claim to the throne, and Charles supported him. Both very publicly turned their backs on the new king and walked out as soon as the crown was placed on his head. Threats were made, and it seems they may have been serious. Their resources and the wizard's power..."

Sir Gareth trailed off ominously. Then, he looked at Aron with sympathy before he spoke again.

"As much as I'd love to spend a few more days here, letting everyone rest and enjoy some home-cooked meals, I'm afraid we need to get to Lanfield and report what we've learned."

That wasn't what Aron wanted to hear, but he supposed he'd have to get used to it if he were to be a knight. Duty came before comfort.

"It may be even worse than you fear." Everyone turned to look at the dragon when he spoke. "I can confirm that the wizard is powerful. You witnessed him knock my dam from the sky with his magic, and that is no small feat. The larger danger, though, is that he is determined to have one of my kind under his control. While she did save us all, my dam's arrival has shown him that there are others out there. I can assure you, if he searches long enough, he will find a dragon willing to help him."

Gareth looked grim at the news. "That's just what we need."

Doubloon inclined his head. "I will help against them, but as you have seen, there are those much more powerful than me. I am still young by dragon standards."

"That settles it, then." The knight turned back to Aron. "Enjoy your family's table this evening. We leave first thing in the morning."

Then, he looked at Skrunt. "All of us."

The koz'thar cowered a little at the idea of being surrounded by so many humans, and the knight softened. "No one will hurt you. That, I promise. You will have the protection of Commander Kyle, the leader of the knights, but he will want to hear the story directly from you."

Gareth's eyes shifted back up to Doubloon. "I don't suppose you would consider joining us, too?"

The dragon dipped his head. "No. I will not expose myself to that many humans. I trust those here, but I know that not all humans are like you. Should the wizard return—and I suspect he will—I will help, but I have no desire to get involved in your politics. If you have need of me, the youngling knows where to find me."

The knight nodded as if he'd expected the answer.

"And now, I think I could use some time in my valley to rest and reflect, so I will take my leave." He turned to Aron. "Do come and visit me when you return."

Doubloon's gaze fell on the koz'thar at the boy's side. The creature who had stood bravely against the dragon's mother now appeared surprisingly uncomfortable with the attention he was getting. "Both of you. I think I should like to get to know our new companion Skrunt better. Any friend of Aron is welcome in my home."

The koz'thar relaxed, and Doubloon smiled.

"I wish you all good luck, and may we meet again soon."

The dragon launched himself into the sky, and Sir Gareth saluted him as he rose and turned back toward his hidden valley. Aron watched his friend go with a bit of sadness. He'd hoped to spend a little more time with Doubloon when no one's life was in danger. He looked forward to when their mission to Lanfield was over, so he could visit the valley again…if his duties as a knight allowed. He considered the possibility that after what he'd done the last few weeks, Gareth might believe him ready to train with the other squires, which would keep him in the city. The thought filled him with a mixture of excitement and dread. He had wanted it for so long, but he had to admit to himself that he wasn't sure if he was ready for it yet.

"Well, we'd best be getting back," his father said. "Caroline will have dinner on the table soon, and we won't want to miss it. Might be the best meal we have for a little while."

Aron sighed and nodded. As Gareth and his father turned to go, Skrunt held him back for a moment. The koz'thar dug around inside his tattered black robes. They'd have to see about fixing those, or better yet, getting him new clothes that no longer tied him to the wizard's army. Maybe his mother could come up with something more suitable. The creature pulled an object from an inner pocket and held it out to the boy. Aron, at first, was taken aback by the circle of strange items —small bones, bird and rat skulls, random pieces of wood—threaded on a rough string. Skrunt nodded toward him.

"Want you have."

Aron shifted his eyes from the disgusting collection to the hopeful look in his friend's face, and under-standing dawned on him. Skrunt was presenting him with the koz'thar version of Doubloon's amulet, and though some of the items on it made him a bit uneasy, he took it with great reverence and placed it around his neck.

He put an arm around the koz'thar's shoulders and pulled him close for a quick hug. Just a couple of years ago, he'd considered dragons and goblins evil creatures for knights to slay, and now, two of them were his best friends. Life was a stranger thing than he'd ever imagined.

"Thank you."

"What friends do," Skrunt said.

Eric and John are teenagers with a plan: buy two scrap freighters, rebuild one, and launch themselves into the stars. Their older sister didn't read the permission slip carefully enough. Now all three are hurtling through the interstellar trade lanes, learning that space is very good at punishing carelessness — and rewarding the stubborn. They'll get conned on their first cargo run, rescue a drifting liner on their second, and discover that even the most harmless-looking passenger can be carrying a gun. Heinlein-style juvenile adventure for boys who'd rather do something than wait to grow up.

Crash Landing by Christopher Nuttall

The second book in the Boy's Own Starship series! Somebody hired the crew of Max Jones to deliver a plague cure to a remote colony. There was no plague. There were, however, pirates waiting in orbit with a very clear plan: take the cargo, take the crew, and leave no witnesses. The attack forces an emergency dive into the atmosphere that ends with Max Jones in pieces in an alien jungle, twenty miles from the nearest settlement, with the ship's medic in a stasis pod and the clock running out. Eric and Vanessa have to walk out. The jungle has opinions about that. So do the pirates. So does whoever set this whole thing up in the first place. Book 2 of the Boys Own Starship Series.

The Weird Map in Mr. Glimm's Skull by Malory

Felix Jones is twelve years old, new in Wild Meadow, and

already hiding in the school boiler room building radios from biscuit tins. It's quieter there. No awkward questions. No stares.

Then he finds the trapdoor.

The one with Russian writing on it.

The school caretaker is gone. Left behind: a brass key, a cryptic note, and a map projected from his own skull by a machine Felix can't explain. And beneath the school, drilled through layers of history and stone, is a Cold War listening post built over something far older. Something vast. Something that has been waiting for exactly the right child to let it out.

It's going to take everything Felix has to make sure he isn't that child.

A full-throttle British adventure. For boys who'd rather be building something than sitting still.

I've Got This! By Frederick Key

Quentin Margolis seems like your average eighth-grader, but he's got a knack for knowing exactly what to bring—whether it's homework, gym clothes, or something as odd as a metal pipe or a flowery umbrella. This quirky ability always saves the day for someone, though it sometimes lands Quentin in a pickle. When his family moves to the small town of Guild River, Quentin's secret talent helps him win over new friends: brainy Jeffrey, wisecracking Kenny, and athletic Thom, son of the police chief. Together, they dive into a thrilling school

project about a decades-old bank heist that left three robbers
dead, one jailed, and a fortune missing.

Fossil Force by Graham Bradley

Patrick Keller, new to the dusty trails of Vina Profunda, Utah,
moves to his grandpa's ranch after tough times hit his family.
On day one, he uncovers an ancient Indian mask that once
belonged to his Uncle Randy. When he slips it on, it sparks a
connection to three local boys—Steve, Tyler, and Howie—
who guard a jaw-dropping secret.As Patrick battles threats in
Utah's wild landscape, he faces tough choices, wrestling with
anger from his family's past. With his friends by his side and
his grandpa's wisdom guiding him, Patrick discovers courage,
teamwork, and the true power of responsibility.

The Tide Runners by Marie-Hélène Lebeault

Beck North grew up watching the tidegate runners — couriers
who carry sealed messages between worlds through
shimmering portals in the harbor. On the day he takes the
runner's oath, Beck inherits his missing father's bronze
tideclock and his first route assignment. Six hours later, he's
outrunning a secret cult in a living coral reef and finding a
symbol that shouldn't exist carved into the walls.

www.ingramcontent.com/pod-product-compliance
Lightning Source LLC
Chambersburg PA
CBHW032221050726

47591CB00001B/206